Message in
MONTANA

Books in the X-Country Adventure series

X - COUNTRY ADVENTURES

Message in
MONTANA

Bob Schaller

Baker Books

A Division of Baker Book House Co
Grand Rapids, Michigan 49516

© 2000 by Bob Schaller

Published by Baker Books
a division of Baker Book House Company
P.O. Box 6287, Grand Rapids, MI 49516-6287

Printed in the United States of America

ISBN 0-8010-4454-5

Library of Congress Cataloging-in-Publication Data is on file at the Library of Congress, Washington, D.C.

While the things the Arlingtons learn about the history, culture, and people of the state are based on actual facts, their adventure itself is fictional.

Historically genuine and correct text relating to the Lewis and Clark expedition was compiled by the National Historical Society from the following resources: Julian P. Boyd, et. al, eds. *The Papers of Thomas Jefferson,* 24 vols. (Princeton, N.J.: Princeton University Press, 1950–90); Donald Jackson, ed. *Letters of the Lewis and Clark Expedition with Related Documents 1783–1854,* 2d ed., 2 vols. (Urbana, Ill.: University of Illinois Press, 1978); Dumas Malone, ed. *Jefferson and His Time,* 6 vols. (Boston: Little, Brown and Company, 1948–81); Gary E. Moulton, ed. *The Journals of the Lewis & Clark Expedition,* 10 vols. (Lincoln: University of Nebraska Press, 1983–96); and Reuben Gold Thwaites, ed., *Original Journals of the Lewis and Clark Expedition, 1804–1806,* 8 vols. (Dodd, Mead, 1904–1905. Reprint, New York: Arno Press, 1969).

For current information about all releases from Baker Book House, visit our web site:

http://www.bakerbooks.com

Contents

A Baffling Board Game

"Dead, at age 35?" Adam Arlington shook his head in disbelief at his mother's statement. "How could that happen? I mean, to a guy that young, and with such a bright future?" Adam's brown eyes were clouded with concern.

"It was a gunshot wound, and to this day, it's unclear whether it was suicide or murder," said Adam's mother, Anne. "There is no question that the explorer Meriwether Lewis led a full life in the short time he was alive." Her short blond curls bobbed as she shook her head for emphasis.

The Arlingtons had spent the morning visiting Montana's capital city—Helena—the first stop on their vacation since setting up camp in Butte. Adam, a lean, blond sixteen-year-old who was entering his junior year at Thomas

Jefferson High School in Washington, D.C., was riding in the front seat of the family's SUV with his mother. Adam's sister, Ashley, a seventeen-year-old eager for her senior year of high school, shared the backseat with her father.

"Hey, here's a coincidence," Ashley said, flipping a lock of long blond hair out of her face. "It says in this Lewis and Clark book that the president who sent them on their way was Meriwether Lewis's good friend, Thomas Jefferson—as in Thomas Jefferson High School!"

"That's pretty neat," Mr. Arlington said. "Jefferson was a great man of his day, and the exploration he chartered changed the nation. There are still a lot of questions surrounding his friend Lewis's death. But one thing is certain: Lewis and Clark and the expedition they led did more for western exploration of the U.S. than anyone ever could have envisioned."

Before long, Mrs. Arlington was pulling into the convenience store near the campground where they'd parked their forty-foot motor home. Butte made a good home base for exploring Montana. Though not exactly in the central part of Montana, Butte would be close to a lot of neat places, including Glacier National Park where the family planned to spend a few days backpacking. Butte also provided easy access to the eastern plains of Montana.

"What do we need for the motor home, Mom?" Adam asked as the SUV rolled to a stop.

"Probably just some milk," Mrs. Arlington answered. "Can you think of anything else, Alex?" she asked her husband. He ran a hand through his brown hair and shook his head.

"We could use a good board game since somebody forgot to pack ours," Ashley said, casting a look at Adam.

"Hey, you could just as easily have packed it yourself," he protested.

"Okay, okay," Mr. Arlington interrupted as Ashley and Adam climbed out of the car. "Get a board game and whatever supplies we need. But no sweets or soda. We have plenty of stuff in the motor home."

The screen door closed with a bang as Adam and Ashley entered the store. The clerk, a tall woman named Kelly, recognized the kids from the day before.

"Back again?" Kelly asked.

"Yes, ma'am," Ashley answered.

"Well, how're you liking Montana?" Kelly inquired.

"If it were up to me, we'd stay all summer," Adam said, smiling. "I really like it here. Washington, D.C. is nice, but there are just so many people, and the traffic is pretty bad. Even though this is only our second day here, I'll bet you we have seen maybe a hundred cars, whereas we'd see that on the road in front of our house in about an hour!"

The three shared a laugh. Ashley picked up a carton of milk and remembered they needed some trash bags, too. She set the items on the counter while Adam lingered in the back of the store.

"Do you have any board games? Monopoly or Clue or something like that?" Adam called to Kelly.

"No, we don't carry games, 'cept for a couple packs of cards here," Kelly answered. "There's a mall and of course we have all the discount chain stores. But you'd have to go about ten miles into town."

Ashley shook her head toward her brother. There was no way their parents would go for a run into town for games, especially since the family always stuck to a strict schedule, and dinnertime was rapidly approaching.

"Wait a minute," Kelly said. "I had an elderly woman— Mrs. Bear Claw, who's about ninety-five years old and has lived in Montana her entire life—come in here a week or so ago, asking if we had a flea market or a store that sold historical items. I told her, 'Sure we do, in town.' But she said she couldn't travel that far and that she was heading to New Mexico by bus to live with relatives. Bus stops right out front here," Kelly said. "And like they say, the road at your feet can take you anywhere you want to go," she added, gesturing toward the parking lot and seeming to lose her train of thought.

"So, what happened?" Ashley prompted.

"Oh, well, the thing of it is, she left a beat-up board game type of thing here with me. Said it was a riddle of sorts, and she was sure someone would want it."

Adam and Ashley looked at each other.

"Interested?" Kelly asked.

"Sure we're interested," Ashley said eagerly, her blue eyes bright with anticipation.

"I really don't know what it's all about," Kelly muttered, rooting around behind the counter. "But I promised her I'd hang onto the thing until someone came looking for it, and you've as good as asked for it so far as I'm concerned. Ah, here we go." She pulled out a flat box and handed it to Adam. "It isn't a traditional board game; it's just a piece of paper and some small trinkets. It had something to do with Lewis and Clark, just a crude drawing, that kind of thing."

"Cool!" Adam exclaimed as he opened the box. "The stuff on the paper is some sort of design. And all the writing on the side was done with those weird, old-fashioned letters."

"And look at these little carved figures," Ashley said, fingering the tiny tokens at the bottom of the box.

Kelly nodded. "I know it's peculiar, but Mrs. Bear Claw told me the box didn't need explaining. I took it off her hands thinking I was only humoring an old woman. But in the bit of time it's been here, I've been dying to know what it all means. And here you come in asking for it, more or less."

Ashley looked inside. "There's all kinds of stuff here," Ashley said. "A couple of cards—except they're made only of paper . . . and they have some sort of trivia or something on them."

"Look," Adam said, "the first one says, 'Left Iceberg' on it. This is kind of bizarre."

"Too bizarre for me," said Kelly. "Like I said, if you want it, it's yours."

Later that evening, after the Arlingtons had cleaned up from dinner and enjoyed a brisk walk around the campground, they sat outside and watched the sun set. But Adam and Ashley were too distracted to savor it.

"Okay, let's have a look at that game you two picked up today," Mrs. Arlington volunteered, sensing her children's anticipation.

"Check this out," Adam said, opening the box to show his parents.

"What is this? It sure doesn't look like Monopoly," Mrs. Arlington observed.

"No, it's about the Lewis and Clark expedition," Ashley said.

"We're not really sure what to make of it yet," Adam said as Ashley nodded in agreement. Adam gingerly opened up the "board," a piece of thick paper folded into fours. "It feels like it's going to break even when you just touch it," he said.

"Is it a map?" Mr. Arlington wondered.

"I think so," Ashley answered, looking at the "board" as her brother flipped it over, trying to make sense of it. The two-foot square of paper had yellowed around the edges. But the colors, which at first glance appeared to form a figure eight, still showed a sense of vibrancy.

Adam pressed open the map, setting small stones on the corners to keep the paper from blowing away. Ashley took the trinkets out of the box. The small wooden figures—not even an inch high—were exquisite under the lantern light.

"Look," Ashley began excitedly. "There's a man . . . two of these are men. And then there's a . . . what is this?"

"It looks like an elk," Mrs. Arlington said, admiring the way the animal's rack, not more than a centimeter high, had been carved with such detail.

"And this?" Adam asked.

"It's a tiny key," his father noted, picking up the small trinket and blowing some dirty cottonlike fiber from the thing.

Ashley and her father looked at the "board" part of the game.

"There's not much to it," Mr. Arlington said.

"That's an understatement," Ashley agreed.

"The pattern kind of looks like a race track, but it couldn't be because it doesn't connect all the way," Adam said. "More like an 'and' sign—an ampersand."

Mrs. Arlington pointed to some small writing in the corner of the paper. "Let's see what we can make of this," she said. She cleared her throat and began to read.

You are here. But "here" is not the answer, although in the end, the finish will be closer to the start than you will be led to believe. The "start" is the point from which you begin, yet it is the beginning you desire. The trail is cold, but the memories are still warm. They will be warmer when you get there. You have questions that I understand. But you will only find answers within the journey. You are the only hope for this quest. There is no shame in declining the challenge. But the reward, achieving the destination, may be well worth your time.

"I don't get it," Adam said, shaking his head.

"Me, neither," his mother agreed.

"Maybe this'll help," Ashley said. She'd pulled a second sheet of aged paper out of the box. "Want me to read it out loud?"

"Sure," Mr. Arlington said as Ashley held the paper up, almost having to squint to read the small letters. Ashley began reading.

In 1803, President Thomas Jefferson won approval from Congress for a project that was to become one of

American history's greatest adventure stories. Jefferson wanted to know if Americans could journey overland to the Pacific Ocean following two rivers, the Missouri and the Columbia, which flow east and west, respectively, from the Rocky Mountains. If the sources of the rivers were nearby, Jefferson reasoned that American traders would have a superior transportation route to help them compete with British fur companies pressing southward from Canada.

On February 28, 1803, Congress appropriated funds for a small U.S. Army unit to explore the Missouri and Columbia rivers and tell the western Indian tribes that traders would soon come to buy their furs. The explorers were to make a detailed report on western geography, climate, plants and animals, and to study the customs and languages of the Indians. Plans for the expedition were almost complete when the president learned that France offered to sell all of Louisiana Territory to the United States. This transfer meant that Jefferson's Army expedition could travel all the way to the crest of the Rockies on American soil, no longer needing permission from the former French owners.

Ashley paused to catch her breath, then continued reading.

Jefferson selected as leader for the exploring mission an Army captain, twenty-eight-year-old Meriwether Lewis. The Jefferson and Lewis families had been neighbors near Charlottesville, Virginia, where Lewis was born August 18, 1774.

Lewis chose a former army comrade, thirty-two-year-old William Clark, to be co-leader of the expedition. Clark was born August 1, 1770, in Caroline County, Virginia. At the age of fourteen, he moved with his family to Kentucky where they were among the earliest settlers.

In preparing for the expedition, Lewis visited the president's scientific friends in Philadelphia for instruction in natural sciences, astronomical navigation, and field medicine. He also was given a long list of questions to ask of western Indians concerning their daily lives.

Lewis and Clark reached their staging point at the confluence of the Mississippi and Missouri rivers near St. Louis in December 1803. The two captains recruited young woodsmen and enlisted soldiers who volunteered from nearby army outposts. In the spring the expedition's roster comprised approximately forty-five, including some military personnel and local boatmen, who would go only partway. Lewis recorded that the camp was "to be considered the point of departure" for the westward journey.

Ashley looked up when she finished reading. "So we have some kind of mission to accept from Mrs. Bear Claw, and here's a record of Lewis and Clark starting their mission." Ashley shrugged. "It's intriguing, but what does it mean?"

Mrs. Arlington held up two cards.

"According to these cards, all we have to go on is 'Left Iceberg' and 'Stone Hills.'" She looked at her husband and children. "Any ideas?"

Adam had been poring through the pages of the travel guide the family had brought to plan their trip.

"If it *is* a kind of riddle, like Kelly told us," he said, "I will wager a guess on the 'Stone Hills' thing."

"And that would be . . ." Ashley said, rolling her hand around as if to say "get on with it."

"Rocky Mountains," Adam answered. "'Stone' could stand for Rocky, and 'Hills' could mean mountains."

"Okay," Ashley said slowly, nodding her head. "Left . . . Iceberg . . . hey, Glacier National Park is up there in the Rocky Mountains! How about West Glacier? Could that work?"

"It's not much to go on, but perhaps it's a start," Mrs. Arlington said.

"Here's the third and final card," said her husband, holding the card under the light.

"What's it say, Dad?" Ashley asked.

"'The Park Ranger.'"

"That's it?" Ashley asked.

Her father held up the card for everyone to see. "That's it. We're heading to Glacier Park anyway. Maybe we can just move the trip up to tomorrow instead of waiting a couple of days until the weekend as we had originally planned," Mr. Arlington suggested.

Mrs. Arlington looked momentarily exasperated. "Honey, it's a giant leap to think that any park ranger—and which park ranger at what park in particular—would know what this is all about," she pointed out.

"I'm up for the challenge," Adam said. "I think there's a lot more to this thing than meets the eye."

"You two are always telling us to keep the 'big picture' in mind," Ashley said, pleading the case.

"Okay, we'll go to Glacier Park in the morning," Mrs. Arlington said. "But remember, we've got a vacation to enjoy! If this thing doesn't pan out, the game is history."

The Quest Begins

The Arlingtons got up the next morning at the crack of dawn and began the day with a brisk jog. When they got back to the motor home, Adam and Mrs. Arlington started loading the SUV while Ashley and her father put together a breakfast of fruits, cereal, and juice.

"You have the tent, the sleeping bags, the camp stove, and all that stuff if we decide to stay up there and camp, right?" Mr. Arlington asked his wife.

"I sure do," she answered. "I'm going to go ahead and pack the cooler and bring some nonperishables just in case we aren't close to a restaurant."

"Good idea," Mr. Arlington said. "From what I read in the travel guide, there are all kinds of places to camp up in Glacier Park."

The Arlingtons headed northwest to Missoula and then went north on a scenic drive through the spectacular Rocky Mountains until they arrived at Glacier National Park. The five-hour drive got the Arlingtons to West Glacier just after noon. The family stopped at a local diner to satisfy their growling stomachs before piling back into the SUV to enter the park. As Mrs. Arlington paid the fee at the West Glacier entrance, she asked where the ranger office for Glacier National Park was located.

The ranger waved them through the gate. "The ranger station is just up the road here," she said with a smile.

The Arlingtons expected the office to be bustling, especially in the summertime, but instead, the office had only a few people in it, perhaps because it was the middle of the week. The large visitors' center had a small, neat display of local wildlife along one wall. An alcove of the main room housed some benches and a large screen. Two rangers, a young man and woman, were busy working behind a desk.

"May I help you folks?" asked the woman.

"We hope so," Mrs. Arlington began. "But it's a long shot."

Ashley explained the finding of the riddle game and the clue cards that had brought the family to the ranger station.

The rangers looked baffled. "I'm sorry," the man said, "but I don't think we can help you."

"Well, it was worth a shot," Mr. Arlington said ruefully. He put an arm around each of his disappointed children. "Let's just put this behind us for now and enjoy the day, okay, kids?" Adam and Ashley smiled weakly.

After thanking the rangers, the Arlingtons walked back to the screening room and sat down to watch the informational video describing Glacier National Park. The four watched breathtaking pictures as the narrator talked about the park's history:

"George Bird Grinnell and others started around 1885 to gain support to organize this area into a national park. Finally, on May 11, 1910, President William H. Taft signed the bill setting this land aside as Glacier National Park," the narrator said.

"Glacier National Park was established to protect the area's spectacular scenic values and the native plant and animal life. The park derives its name from the more than thirty glaciers found here. The park encompasses approximately 1.4 million acres of wilderness and some of the most beautiful mountain scenery in the western United States. A combination of spectacular scenery, diverse flora and fauna, and relative isolation from major population centers have combined to make Glacier National Park the center of one of the largest and most intact ecosystems in North America. The general park area was once the homeland of the Blackfoot and Kootenai Indian tribes, and many sites in the park are sacred spiritual sites."

"Interesting," Mrs. Arlington said as the video continued. "There's certainly a lot of history here."

"Yeah, I just wish we could track down a little more recent history, like Mrs. Bear Claw's train of thought," Adam said, dejected.

"Look, I know you're disappointed, Adam," said his mother, "but we're still getting what we came for—vacation. Come on, we haven't lost anything. We gave Mrs. Bear Claw's mystery a try, and we're none the worse for it. Let's cheer up, okay, kiddo?"

"Okay, okay," Adam sulked.

The video ended and the Arlingtons rose to leave the screening room. As they walked past the display area toward the exit, Ashley stopped short.

"Look!" she cried. "It's her! It's Mrs. Bear Claw!"

Ashley stared at the photo gallery wall, on which was mounted an eight-by-ten picture of an old Indian woman speaking before a rapt audience. The caption read, "Sarah Bear Claw spellbinds listeners at our annual storytelling retreat."

"That has to be our Mrs. Bear Claw!" Ashley said excitedly.

Adam stepped back to the front desk. "Are there any other rangers who work here?" he asked the two rangers they'd spoken to earlier.

"Sure," one said. He smiled and pointed to the door. "As a matter of fact, here comes the boss, back from lunch!"

A pleasant-looking woman of about forty stepped through the doors at that moment. "Somebody has business with the boss?" she asked cheerfully.

Mrs. Arlington explained the riddle game again to the senior ranger, Rebecca Kinnison, and asked if she knew the old woman in the photo.

"Sure do," Rebecca answered. "Sarah Bear Claw used to give talks here up until a few years ago," she explained. "Recently she'd become a bit too infirm to make the trip, sad to say. I've missed her," she said, shaking her head sadly. "These two youngsters haven't been here long enough to have known her or heard her wonderful stories," she added, indicating the other two rangers.

"So you do know her; that's a step in the right direction," Ashley said with enthusiasm.

"Yeah, and strange as it may seem, I got an envelope with her name on the return address just the other day." Adam and Ashley shared an excited look between them. "I haven't even opened it yet, to tell you the truth," Rebecca went on. "Why don't you come on back to my office and we'll have a look together."

"Fantastic!" Ashley said.

After flipping through most of a pile of in-box items, Rebecca unearthed a small manila envelope and slit it open. In it were a folded piece of paper and a card the same size and shape as the three from the riddle game; clearly it was another clue card.

The ranger held up the card. "It says, 'of largess and not standing. Look for history. Nothing more. Good luck!'" Rebecca looked up and smiled apologetically. "Cryptic, isn't it?"

The others agreed.

Rebecca unfolded the sheet of paper. "Let's see . . . a note says, 'You will know when the right people appear to request this. Please send them forward.'"

Ashley and Adam smiled. "That's us," Adam said eagerly.

Rebecca chuckled. "The rest of this looks to be a description of part of the Lewis and Clark expedition—want me to read aloud?" she asked.

"Yes, please," Adam answered.

"Okay, here goes," Rebecca started to read.

The Lower Missouri:
May 14, 1804 to April 1805

The expedition broke camp on May 14, 1804. Clark wrote in his journal: "I set out at 4 o'clock p.m. . . . and proceeded on under a gentle breeze up the Missouri." The party traveled in a fifty-five-foot long keelboat and two smaller boats called "pirogues." Through the long, hot summer they worked their way upriver. Numerous hazards, including sunken trees called "sawyers," sandbars, *collapsing riverbanks, and sudden squalls of high winds with drenching rains slowed their progress.*

There were other problems, including disciplinary floggings, two desertions, a man dishonorably discharged for mutiny, and the apparent appendicitis-caused death of Sgt. Charles Floyd, the only member to die during the expedition. In what is now the state of South Dakota, a band of Teton Sioux tried to detain the boats, but the explorers showed their superior armaments and sailed on.

Early in November they came to the villages of the Mandan and Minitari (Hidatsa) Indians, who lived near present-day Washburn, North Dakota. On the north bank of the Missouri River they found a grove of stout cottonwood trees of the proper size for construction of a log fort.

"Okay," Ashley interrupted. "North Dakota is the state to the east of Montana, right? So they're not even in Montana yet?"

"Who cares? What are you, our walking atlas?" Adam said, giving his sister a light poke in the arm.

"Kids, come on—let Ranger Kinnison continue!" their mother said, cautioning them with a look. The ranger went on:

Standing close together, the trees also offered protection from the prairie winds. In four weeks of hard work the men built a triangular-shaped fort. They named it Fort Mandan in honor of the local inhabitants. The party was

now 164 days and approximately 1,510 miles distant
from where they began at Camp Wood.

The explorers spent five months at Fort Mandan, hunting
and obtaining information about the route ahead from the
Indians and French-Canadian traders who lived nearby. The
expedition's blacksmiths set up a forge and made tools and
implements, which were traded for the Indians' garden crops
of corn, melons, and beans.

A French-Canadian named Toussaint Charbonneau
visited the captains with his young pregnant Shoshone wife,
Sacagawea. Sacagawea's tribal homeland lay in the Rocky
Mountain country far to the west. She had been kidnapped
by Plains Indians five years previously when she was about
twelve years old and was taken to the North Dakota villages
where she was eventually sold to Charbonneau.

"Wait a second—you mean she was only my age?" Again
Ashley interrupted.

"And you thought you were pretty cool just being a star
basketball player," Adam teased.

Ranger Kinnison smiled and continued reading.

Sacagawea spoke both Shoshone and Minitari, and the
captains realized that she could be a valuable
intermediary if the party encountered the Shoshones.
Moreover, Sacagawea would prove to be a token of truce,
assuring the Indians that the expedition was peaceful.
Clark later documented this while descending the
Columbia River when he noted, "No woman ever
accompanies a war party of Indians in this quarter." The

captains hired Charbonneau, who was joined by
Sacagawea and their infant son, Jean Baptiste
Charbonneau. The boy became a favorite of Clark, who
nicknamed him "Pomp," citing his pompous "little
dancing boy" antics.

The ranger finished reading, looked up, and smiled. "Interesting," she said.

"Interesting, and confusing," Mrs. Arlington added. "I have no idea what all this means or what it has to do with Montana."

"Well, you know Lewis and Clark accomplished most of Jefferson's mandates right here in Montana—they discovered umpteen plants and animals that were new to science, and they had lots of dealings with Native Americans here," Ranger Kinnison explained. "We're very big on the Lewis and Clark expedition in Montana," she added. "If you like, I could point out some areas of interest to Lewis and Clark fans."

"We've already taken up too much of your time," Mrs. Arlington said, extending her hand to Ranger Kinnison.

"Well, I wish I could give you more information," Kinnison said, "but that 'clue' means nothing more to me than it does to you. All I know is, Mrs. Bear Claw is a very wise person with a real sense of the land and the people. If she's sent you on a kind of quest, then I'd say pursuing it is worth your while."

Cracking the Code

The Arlingtons spent the rest of the afternoon driving along the park's Going-to-the-Sun Road before enjoying a leisurely drive back to Butte. They saw stunning views of the mountains and valleys of Glacier National Park, stopped for a quick tour of the city of Missoula, and enjoyed watching a gorgeous setting sun paint the clouds pink. It was near midnight when the Arlingtons finally got back to the campground. It had been a long day but a thought-provoking one in terms of Mrs. Bear Claw's riddle game.

Mr. and Mrs. Arlington, who had split the driving duties, announced that they were ready to call it a day and headed for their room in the back of the motor home. Though it was late, Ashley and Adam went to sit outside under the motor home's awning since the temperature was still around sixty-five degrees.

"This might not be like our other trips," Ashley said to Adam, pulling an afghan around her shoulders. "I mean, really, this mystery might be over before it starts."

"You sound like Mom."

"She just doesn't want us to be disappointed, that's all, Adam. I don't want to be disappointed either," Ashley admitted.

"I know—but it was sort of miraculous that we hooked up with Ranger Rebecca on the first try, wasn't it?"

"Almost the first try," Ashley reminded her brother. "We were this close to leaving with nothing, remember?" She held her thumb and forefinger a smidgen apart.

Ashley pulled her atlas out of her backpack. Rather than moving his chair over toward his sister, Adam opened his laptop computer and turned it on. He had a map program on it, which he often used either to plan or follow the family's trips.

"I see the Rocky Mountains, an Indian reservation, and lots of other stuff," Ashley said. "And nothing has anything to do with 'of largess' or 'not standing.'"

Adam moved his cursor around the map of Montana. He, too, saw nothing that seemed to connect to the clues they'd picked up that day at Glacier National Park.

"It seems hopeless," Ashley said dejectedly.

"Listen, Ash," Adam said. "Obviously, that card was part of the riddle game, right? And to the person who made this game, there was something important at stake. How can we give up so soon?"

"That's a good question," Ashley wondered. "But I have a better one."

"And that question," Adam said, "is what?"

"How can we go any further if we have nothing else to go on?" Ashley said.

Ashley ran her finger along the Montana border in the west with Idaho and then did the same thing on the east Montana border where the state meets North Dakota. "I'm going to call it a day," Ashley said, shaking her head in frustration. "I'm beat, and you know Mom and Dad won't cut us much slack in the morning; they'll still have us up for a run or bike ride at the crack of dawn."

Adam didn't answer, looking along the Front Range of the Rocky Mountains into west-central Montana.

"Stay put for a second," Adam said excitedly. "The clues—tell me them again."

"One was 'of largess,' and the other was 'not standing.'"

Adam bobbed his head up and down.

"What is it, Adam?" Ashley asked. "You look like you just found a four-leaf clover."

"Better than that," Adam said. "I think I have an idea of what's going on. Hmmmm."

"Come on, tell me!" Ashley demanded, standing up to look over Adam's shoulder at his computer screen.

"Hang on, let me back into this so I can make sure I'm not totally off base," Adam said. "First of all, would 'of largess' mean, at least theoretically, that something is 'great'?"

"I could buy that—yeah, 'great' would fit," Ashley said. "Is that it?"

"Okay," Adam said. "And if something is 'not standing,' could we say that it has 'fallen' in some way, shape, or form?"

"'Great Fallen' is what you came up with?" Ashley asked her brother incredulously. "What does that have to do with anything?"

"Not 'Great Fallen,'" Adam said. "Look here, northeast of Helena—"

Adam pointed at a dot on his computer screen.

"Great Falls!" Ashley said.

Adam ran his fingers through his hair.

"But where in Great Falls, who in Great Falls?" Adam asked.

"'Look for history. Nothing more,'" Ashley said again, looking at the card Rebecca had given them.

"That doesn't mean much to me," Adam said. "At least nothing that I can think of right now."

"Maybe Mom and Dad will have some thoughts in the morning," Ashley said. "Let's go inside. It's getting chilly out here."

They started up the stairs back into the motor home.

"At least we've made a start," Adam observed. "Tomorrow I bet we'll crack this case wide open."

Ashley laughed quietly. "You mean today, don't you?" she said, pointing to the clock on the wall. "We'd better get some sleep. Mom and Dad have been in bed for over an hour. They're going to wipe us out in the morning run."

"Okay, Ash," Adam said. "But I sure am excited about Great Falls."

"Well, the only thing I'm worried about 'not standing' in the next ten seconds is me," Ashley said, and with that she flopped down on her bed.

Adam and Ashley misjudged their parents—Mr. and Mrs. Arlington let them sleep in a little in the morning. But their mother led the run and kept a pace that even

Adam—a two-year letterman on the Thomas Jefferson High cross-country team—struggled to keep up with that morning. The four got back to the motor home and ate breakfast as Ashley and Adam filled their parents in on what they had figured out late the night before.

"That's good stuff, you two," Mrs. Arlington said after Adam explained their answer to the riddle. "I'm up for a trip to Great Falls. We can see if there are any museums there, for a start. We'll play it by ear; maybe we can get a grasp on the second part of the clue once we're in town."

The drive from Butte to Great Falls was as pretty as the drive the day before. The family passed through miles and miles of national forest and rolled into Great Falls late morning.

Their first stop was the Chamber of Commerce office, where Mrs. Arlington explained to a bewildered employee their reason for being in Great Falls. The employee couldn't help them but suggested they try visiting the Lewis and Clark Interpretive Center. So they hopped back in the SUV and drove along River Drive to the Center.

The impressive building was built into the rock, overlooking the Missouri River, and housed all kinds of exhibits about the expedition. Adam tried his luck with the test-of-strength exhibit, where visitors pull a rope to see how far they can drag a canoe upstream. After watching a short documentary on the Lewis and Clark journey, the Arlingtons sought out several staff members and showed them all their clue cards. But they met with no luck and no shortage of blank stares.

"I have an idea," Ashley said, stepping lightly down the steps of the building. "When I did a paper in school last year, I had to call up to this small town in New England. The lady at the local library referred me to the town's historical society director, and he helped me find the information I needed to finish my paper."

"Good thought, Ash," her mother said, nodding. After checking for the address in the phone book, the Arlingtons walked a couple of blocks to the building that housed the historical society. Inside, they were greeted by a young man wearing a name tag that said "Tim."

"We're looking for the historical society director," Mr. Arlington began.

"Oh, well, I'm just interning here for the summer," Tim said. "I can go get the director if you want. Could I tell her what this is about?"

"You bet," Mrs. Arlington said. "We're looking for a needle in a very large haystack."

Tim looked puzzled. Mrs. Arlington smiled and continued.

"This is going to sound strange, but we're looking for a card like this one," she said, showing Tim the card that had brought them to Great Falls.

"We're following a sort of riddle game," Ashley explained to the baffled intern. "The first clue card took us to West Glacier. The clue we found in West Glacier brought us here."

Tim threw his hands in the air. "This one's a little beyond me," he said good-naturedly. "Mrs. Simon hasn't taught me anything about mysterious clue cards yet," he added. "She's the director, Karen Simon. Let me go see if she's available to talk with you. Be right back."

Tim disappeared down a hall, and the Arlingtons began to poke around the display area.

"I have a good feeling about this," Ashley said. "If you think about it, the historical society's the only logical answer to the clue—'look for history, nothing more'—the other stops we made weren't purely historical, they were also contemporary."

Her musings were interrupted by Karen Simon's entrance into the room. It seemed too good to be true, but she was holding an envelope in her hand.

After introductions all around, Mrs. Simon fluttered the envelope in the air. "I think this might be what you're looking for," she said. "May I see the information you have?"

"Actually, we didn't bring all of it," Ashley said. "We have a big piece of paper, and it looks like the board part of a board game." Ashley showed Mrs. Simon the cards. "This card says 'Left Iceberg' on it, which we figured out meant West Glacier." She told her how Ranger Kinnison had helped them at Glacier National Park and how Adam had decoded the second clue that read "of largess and not standing."

"And that's what brought us to Great Falls," Ashley finished. "The riddle game has something to do with the Lewis and Clark expedition—a paper telling about the beginning of their trip came with the game, and the ranger gave us a description of another leg of the journey along with the second clue."

"Well, Great Falls marked a tough time in the journey, I can tell you that," Mrs. Simon began. "It took them a month to get around the falls. But this'll tell you more," she said, pulling out a tattered, folded piece of paper and handing it to Ashley. "It's about the Great Falls Portage, and like you, I got this in the mail along with my cards."

"May I have the honors?" Ashley asked with a grin. She quickly began to read.

The Upper Missouri: April 1805 to July 1805

Moving up the river from the Mandan villages, they passed the confluence of the Yellowstone with the Missouri and entered a country where Lewis observed "immense herds of buffalo, elk, deer & antelope feeding in one common and boundless pasture." Grizzly bears charged the men hunting them. Lewis commented that he would "rather fight two Indians than one bear." River navigation became more difficult. During a fierce windstorm, the pirogue that carried important records and instruments began filling with water and nearly capsized. Sacagawea, who was aboard, saved many items as they floated within her reach. Near the end of May, the great Rocky Mountains came into view. The river's current grew stronger. The explorers had to abandon the paddles and tow the heavy canoes with rawhide ropes while walking along the shoreline. When riverbanks gave way to cliffs, the men had to wade in the water, pushing and pulling the boats upstream.

"Wow—that's hard! I know from the test-of-strength exhibit at the Interpretive Center!" Adam interrupted. "But I could've done it," he said when Ashley shot him a look. Ashley continued.

In early June, the explorers reached a point where the Missouri seemed to divide equally into northerly and southerly branches. Here they spent nine days concluding that the south branch was the true Missouri. Lewis named the north fork the Marias River and scouted ahead with a small advance party following the south fork until he heard waterfalls. The Indians at Fort Mandan had told them about the falls of the Missouri, so Lewis knew he was on the right stream.

Here, in the vicinity of present-day Great Falls, Montana, the expedition had to portage eighteen miles around a series of five cascades of the Missouri. The men attached cottonwood wheels to the canoes to push them over land. The weather was hot with intermittent squalls pelting the party with large, bruising hailstones. Transporting the heavy boats and baggage up the steep incline from the river and traversing the long stretch of prairie lands was an exhausting ordeal. Prickly pear spines penetrated their feet through moccasin soles, adding to the difficult and fatiguing travel. "Good or bad, we must make the portage," Lewis wrote of the situation.

"Sounds like quite an ordeal," Mr. Arlington marveled when Ashley had finished reading. Mrs. Simon opened the envelope again and pulled out two small cards, identical in size and shape to the other clue cards. One read "Half the team and city." The second read, "Two heads see eye to eye."

There was a brief silence while everyone considered these new clues.

"May I offer a suggestion?" Mrs. Simon asked.

"We're big on taking any and all suggestions," Mr. Arlington answered with a grin.

"If this whole thing has to do with Lewis and Clark, maybe 'Half the team' has something to do with Lewis or Clark," the director offered.

"That's a good thought," Adam said. "Is there a Clark City or a Lewis City?"

Just then, Tim interrupted. "Excuse me, Mrs. Simon, the aide to the senator is on the phone for your conference call."

"That's right! I lost track of the time," the director said. "I'll be tied up until after lunch, but you folks are welcome to this card, and you're also welcome to come back sometime after lunch if you'd like."

"Oh, no, we'll be on our way," Mrs. Arlington said. "Thanks so much for your time."

"Will you let me know if you find something else or how this thing ends?" Mrs. Simon asked over her shoulder as she hurried back to her office.

A second later Adam groaned. "We didn't even find out her connection to Mrs. Bear Claw!"

Tim spoke up again then. "That's a familiar name. Can't imagine that wouldn't be the same person. I mean, how many Mrs. Bear Claws could there be?"

Dead-End

By now the sun was high in the early afternoon sky, and the temperature had soared. The four Arlingtons stood around staring at the card Adam now held in his hand.

"I can't figure this one out," his father admitted, scratching his head.

"Wait a minute," Ashley said. She'd pulled out the road map and was running her finger along the routes. "How does 'Lewistown' sound? 'Lewis' for 'Half the team' and 'town' for 'City.'"

"That's it!" Adam said.

Ashley slumped her shoulders.

"For someone who just put us on our way, you don't look too happy," Mrs. Arlington said to Ashley.

"Well, I'm glad that we have another town to visit," Ashley said. "But that's all we have. This time, we don't have a contact person—a park ranger or historical society director—we don't have anybody to get in touch with when we get there. I just don't get the second part of this clue at all."

"Cheer up, Ashley," encouraged her mother. "We'll keep plugging away, okay? Good or bad, we'll 'make the portage,' right?"

The Arlingtons headed out of Great Falls and stopped several miles out of town on a side road that had an old bridge just off the Missouri River. Mrs. Arlington pulled out a few sandwiches she'd put together that morning before leaving the campground, and everyone sat down on a blanket Mr. Arlington spread out on the grassy ground.

Adam studied the road map. "We're looking at about 110 miles east on U.S. 87 to get to Lewistown," he said.

"That doesn't sound overwhelming," Mrs. Arlington said. "I think we can do it quite easily."

"But we're also talking about almost 250 miles back to the motor home in Butte when we're done," Adam said.

Mrs. Arlington shook her head. "No, it's okay, we don't have to go back," she insisted. "We packed all the camping gear for yesterday's trip. We need to fill the cooler, but aside from that, we're all set."

"So, is it off to Lewistown?" Mr. Arlington asked.

"Let's go," Mrs. Arlington answered.

Ashley and Adam smiled at each other, glad that their parents shared their enthusiasm for the challenge they'd stumbled on.

Soon the Arlingtons were nearing Lewistown. Just before they reached the town, they saw directions to a campground in the Lewis and Clark National Forest among the Big Snowy Mountains just south of town.

"We can set up camp after we head into town," Mrs. Arlington said.

Mr. Arlington agreed. "Maybe we can even fish for dinner if we find a good spot," he added.

"I see a lake on the map on the northwest edge of the forest," Adam said. "That's also where a campground is. This could be fun."

The family had no idea where to start in Lewistown. Since it was nearing five o'clock, they figured they'd better find out what they could as soon as possible, before the close of the business day.

They parked in town and purposefully walked the length of the main street. They saw a café, a library building, and signs directing them to a school and a recreation area, but nothing seemed to fit. Near the east entrance to town, the family sat on a street-corner bench in silence.

Adam's gaze drifted to the Lewis and Clark Trading Post, which stood in an old two-story building on the southwest corner of the block. Caricatures of Lewis and Clark were painted on a large billboard, which appeared to be as old as the building itself.

"Two heads see eye to eye . . ." Adam murmured. "Come on!" he suddenly shouted, hopping up from the bench. Adam crossed the street at the corner, pointing up at the faces of Lewis and Clark on the billboard. "You get it?" he asked his family, following close behind.

"Good eye, Adam!" Ashley said. "Two heads—two explorers on the sign."

"I would have gotten it right off if the clue had read 'eye to eye to eye to eye,'" their father joked, as they pushed open the double doors to the trading post. A red and white "open" sign invited the Arlingtons inside. A young girl behind a counter was talking to a teenage friend. She turned to them and smiled.

"Hi," the girl said. "Welcome to Lewis and Clark Trading Post. Can I help you find something, or are you just exploring?"

Adam explained that they were on vacation from the East Coast, and that what they were looking for would sound kind of odd. "We're following a kind of riddle game with wooden game pieces and clue cards having to do with Lewis and Clark. Does any of this seem—"

"Oh, you are the people she was talking about!" the girl interrupted, waving her hands excitedly. "I remember when something came in the mail a few days ago—a clue, I guess! Martha didn't have any idea what it meant, but I know the thing said somebody would come asking about it."

"So, Martha is somebody who works here?" Ashley asked.

"Yeah, Martha Miller—she owns the place," the clerk answered. "Too bad she's not around because I'm sure she really would have liked to meet you."

"Excuse me?" Adam asked. "What do you mean, she 'would have liked' to meet us?"

"She just left, not even fifteen minutes ago, for the airport," the girl said. "She's going on vacation for the next three weeks."

"Three weeks!" Ashley exclaimed. "We'll be long gone by then! I know this is asking a lot, and you don't know us or anything, but could you let us see the clue you got in the mail?"

The clerk shook her head. "I'm so sorry," she said. "She keeps a lot of papers in her desk upstairs, but her office is locked. And I'm afraid she has the only key."

"Did she leave a number where we could reach her?" Ashley asked.

"Actually, no," the clerk said. "But when she gets there in a couple days, she'll call her son—he's going to manage the place for her while she's gone—with a number in Hawaii."

"Hawaii?" Adam asked. "We're sunk."

"I wish I could help you," the girl said. "I just feel terrible, seeing the looks on your faces."

"That's how life is, and we'll take the ups and downs and remain on an even keel," Mrs. Arlington said.

"Well, take care," the clerk said. "And good luck."

The Arlingtons walked out through the big swinging doors and stood staring at each other for a moment.

"No clue, no more steps forward for us," Adam said finally.

"I'm afraid you're right," Mrs. Arlington said.

Mr. Arlington forced a smile. "Hey, I saw a store two blocks down," he said. "What do you say we walk down there for some extra camp food, okay? Maybe we can find some delicious dehydrated dessert we can whip up on the camp stove later," he said, trying to muster up some enthusiasm.

The four walked slowly down the clean sidewalk to the store and bought some rolls, a couple of boxes of macaroni and cheese, and a package of cookies, along with some fruit and juice and a few other items they could prepare simply in camp.

"You know, we've already been able to see a few places we hadn't planned on seeing when we set out for Montana," Mr. Arlington told the kids in the checkout line, trying to perk them up.

"Yes, and we've also met some people we wouldn't have otherwise met," Mrs. Arlington said. "I think we can do some serious fishing and hiking tonight and tomorrow. In fact, we can stay an extra day and camp tomorrow night too, if you want to. There's a lot of other stuff to see in this area. Let's go back to the car and head to the campground. We'll check out the travel guide and brochures and see what other exciting things we can find. I'm sure there are literally a million things to do."

"But not what we set out for," Ashley said quietly.

"Yeah, I kind of feel like heading back to the motor home and just picking up the trip like this whole thing never happened," Adam said.

"That's not an attitude I often see from either one of you," Mrs. Arlington said. "Chin up, and let's get on with our vacation. Really, what could we have hoped for from this mystery?"

"I don't know, Mom," Ashley said. "But at least something more than this."

Mr. Arlington smiled.

"You almost sound greedy, kids," he said. "Come on, we're always talking about how things are what we make them—nothing more and nothing less. Now, if you really want to believe that this vacation is going to be a letdown from here on out, then it probably will be. On the other hand, if you want to be a little more mature about it and regain your perspective, we can make this another terrific vacation."

Ashley sighed. "You're right, Dad," she said.

"Sorry we're acting like babies about it," Adam agreed.

"It's okay," Mr. Arlington said. "It's a disappointment for all of us."

They were walking back to the car when they saw the clerk out in front of the Lewis and Clark Trading Post, talking animatedly to a woman. The girl was raising her hands with obvious emotion. Mr. Arlington took a couple of quick strides.

"Hello!" Mr. Arlington shouted. "Is everything all right?"

"That's them!" the girl exclaimed to the woman beside her. "That's them, Mrs. Miller—the people I told you about who were just here!"

Back in the Game

"Talk about good luck," Martha Miller said, after introducing herself and the clerk, whose name was Cathy. "My flight to Helena was postponed because of a problem with the charter. It's not a big deal—I didn't connect until tomorrow from Helena to Salt Lake City anyway. But from what Cathy is telling me, I'm glad I ended up having my plans unexpectedly changed."

The Arlingtons could hardly believe what was happening.

"Why don't you wait out here," Martha suggested. "I'll get the envelope from my office, and we can sit out here on the benches and go over it together. It's such a nice evening that I'd hate to waste any more of it inside."

Adam retrieved their riddle game material from the car, and when Martha came outside again, they all sat down together.

"I have this piece of paper—it almost looks like a playing card," Martha said. "The only reason I hung onto it was that it was so peculiar. And whoever sent it to me, this

Sarah Bear Claw, sounds so earnest in her note about waiting for somebody who'll come looking for this stuff. What do you all have?"

"We've found clue after clue leading us from place to place," Ashley said. "The most recent clue was given to us in Great Falls, and it led us straight to you."

"Well, I wouldn't call the path *straight*, Ash," Adam said. Everyone laughed.

Mrs. Arlington explained the clue that had made them stop at the trading post. Cathy smiled shyly when Mrs. Arlington mentioned how attentive the clerk had been.

Martha reached into the envelope and pulled out a small piece of paper.

"Well, here it is. All I have is this, and it doesn't make a lot of sense to me," she said.

Taped to the paper—which had no writing on it at all—was a newspaper clipping profiling the reenactment of Custer's Last Stand, staged each year at what is now the Crow Agency on the reservation. "Like I said, it's not much to go on, but it is something." She handed the clipping to Ashley.

"This lists several dates the reenactment will be staged this month—there's one the day after tomorrow," Ashley said. She held the paper clipping up and noticed an indent in the paper. "Someone's underlined 'General Custer.'"

The Arlingtons looked at each other. "No history lesson with this clue," Adam observed. "So are we headed to the reenactment, Dad?"

"I guess so," Mr. Arlington replied. "We're off to see General Custer!"

"I can't believe it!" Ashley said. "Thank you for all your help, Mrs. Miller. We're so very glad we ended up meeting you."

"Thanks, the pleasure was mine," Martha said. "Will you do me a favor and drop me a line about how this turns out?"

"We sure will," Ashley said, accepting a business card from Martha Miller.

The Arlingtons got back into the car, and Ashley, who was driving to give her parents a break, started to back out.

"Wait!" Mrs. Arlington cried out.

Ashley put on the brakes and saw Martha rushing at them waving something in her hand. Ashley put her window down.

"Yes, ma'am?" Ashley asked.

"I can't believe I almost forgot this," Mrs. Miller said, handing the paper to Ashley. "Mrs. Bear Claw also included a phone number of where she can be reached in New Mexico. Apparently, she just moved from Montana recently."

The Arlingtons perked up in a hurry. To get in touch with Mrs. Bear Claw could fill in a lot of blanks.

When they got to the campground, Mrs. Arlington dialed the number as her family stood by, watching intently.

Anne Arlington explained that she was a history professor in Washington, D.C., in Montana on vacation. Then she shared how her family had been given some clues Mrs. Bear Claw left behind before she headed to New Mexico. She asked if she could speak with Mrs. Bear Claw.

Mrs. Arlington had been leaning casually against the wall as she talked. Suddenly, she stood straight up and held the phone with both hands.

"My goodness!" Mrs. Arlington said. "I'm sorry to bother you. . . . I understand. . . . How? . . . Our prayers are with you. . . ."

Adam and Ashley desperately wanted to find out what their mom had just been told.

Mrs. Arlington cupped one hand over the phone, and in a whisper, cured their curiosity: "Mrs. Bear Claw," she said quietly, "died two days ago."

"Sure," Mrs. Arlington said as she prepared to hang up the phone after a few more moments of conversation. "No, we did not know that. But that certainly helps us understand why Mrs. Bear Claw was so interested in this. . . . A fax? We can see if the campground hosts have one; if not, I'm sure we can find one in town tomorrow and give you a call with the number. . . . Yes, I understand, and we'll call you when—or if—we figure this thing out. . . . No, really, we will be in touch. God bless you, and I hope your family pulls through this all right. Your grandmother obviously had a very active mind all the way up until the end—we're learning quite a bit from her even now."

Mrs. Arlington finished up the conversation, then found that the campground hosts did indeed have a fax machine and arranged for the fax to go through.

"That's pretty sad," Adam said as they waited for the fax. "It's just too bad she died."

"It really is," Mrs. Arlington said. "But she died in her sleep of natural causes."

"What did they tell you about why Mrs. Bear Claw made this riddle up in the first place?" Ashley asked her mother.

"It turns out Mrs. Bear Claw was a descendant of Sacagawea," Mrs. Arlington said. "In fact, she had that for a middle name, Sacagawea."

"So, what's coming in on the fax?" Mr. Arlington asked.

"Apparently, Mrs. Bear Claw told her family nothing about the riddle, except that she had forgotten to include something," Mrs. Arlington said. "She worried up to the hours before she died about how important it was for this piece of paper to get to whoever found her 'game.' It's some more Lewis and Clark information."

"I was all ready to give this thing up for a while there," Ashley said. "Now I feel like we have to keep going with it for Mrs. Bear Claw. We're her only chance."

"I'm glad we're on this quest of yours, too," Mr. Arlington agreed.

A beep indicated the end of the fax transmission. Mrs. Arlington tore the paper cleanly, then put on her glasses and began to read.

West of the Divide: July 1805 to November 1805

On July 25, the expedition arrived at a place where the Missouri divided into three forks. The southeast branch they named the Gallatin for the secretary of the treasury. The southerly one was named the Madison for the secretary of state. The westerly branch became the Jefferson River "in honor of that illustrious personage Thomas Jefferson, President of the United States." Because it flowed from the west, the captains decided to follow the Jefferson.

Learning from Sacagawea that they were now within traditional food-gathering lands of her people, Lewis went ahead of the main party seeking the Shoshones. In the middle of August he reached a spring in the mountains that he called "the most distant fountain" of the Missouri. Just beyond was a saddle in a high ridge (today's Lemhi

Pass), from which Lewis saw towering, snow-covered mountains to the west. A brook at his feet ran westward, and he knew he had crossed the Continental Divide. The brook was one of many tributary streams of today's Snake River, which in turn joins the Columbia.

Immediately west of the Continental Divide, Lewis came upon two Shoshone women and a girl who were digging edible roots. Lewis gave them presents, and soon they were joined by a large number of Shoshone men on horseback. Returning from this scouting trip accompanied by a number of Shoshones, Lewis rejoined Clark and the main party. The explorers formed a camp with the Indians a few miles south of present-day Dillon, Montana, which they named "Camp Fortunate." Here, Sacagawea found a long-lost childhood girlfriend. The girl had been with Sacagawea when both were captured, but had escaped and returned to her people. Sacagawea learned that her own brother, Cameahwait, was now chief of the tribe. It was an emotional scene when brother and sister were reunited.

"Wow! I can't imagine what that would be like," interrupted Adam. His mother continued reading.

Thinking ahead to the return journey, Captain Lewis ordered the canoes submerged to "guard against both the effects of high water and that of fire . . . the Indians promised to do them no intentional injury." The party then proceeded across the Continental Divide to the main village of the Shoshones. With Sacagawea as interpreter, a

Shoshone guide was hired, and trading with the Indians for riding horses and packhorses was successful. After a short stay with their new friends, the now horse-mounted corps followed their guide, Old Toby, into the "formidable mountains."

September found the half-starved explorers surviving on horse meat while following an ancient Indian route, the Lolo Trail, across the Bitterroot Mountains in modern Montana and Idaho. Here, they encountered fallen timber, bone-chilling cold, and slippery, hazardous travel during an early season snowstorm. Descending the west slope of the mountains, they reached a village of the Nez Perce, where the natives provided a feast of salmon, roots, and berries. The ravenous explorers found to their dismay that this diet made them extremely ill.

The group reached today's Clearwater River where they branded and left their horses in the care of the Nez Perce until their return. They built new canoes and proceeded through boulder-strewn rapids, making speedy but risky progress. In early October they reached the Snake River and then on October 16, the Columbia.

On November 2, they drifted into the quiet upper reaches of tidewater on the Columbia. Clark, on November 7, wrote: "great joy in camp; we are in view of the ocean, this great Pacific Ocean which we have been so long anxious to see." They were still twenty-five miles upstream, and what they actually saw were the storm-lashed waves of the river's broad estuary. For the next nine days savage winds blew, ocean swells rolled into the river, *and the rain poured down, stranding them in unprotected camps just above the tide at the base of cliffs. In mid-November the captains finally strode upon the sands of the Pacific Ocean near the Columbia's mouth, the western objective of their journey. Clark recorded that 554 days had elapsed, and 4,132 miles had been traveled since leaving Camp Wood.*

The Arlingtons looked at each other.

"So we're at the end of the expedition route," Mrs. Arlington said. "Pretty exciting stuff! If I remember my history, Captain Clark finds a beached whale not long after the party reaches the Pacific."

Mr. Arlington laughed. "Well, we can rule out finding a whale at the end of our little expedition. But let's hope we find something equally magnificent!"

Meeting Custer

The family broke into pairs for that evening's fishing competition. It was a family tradition to team up for fishing contests—winners shared the spoils of victory, but not the dish duty. Mrs. Arlington and Adam reeled in a couple of medium-sized catfish while Ashley pulled in a large trout.

"Since I was the one shut out—not even a bite!—I'll clean the fish and do the cooking," Mr. Arlington said. "Adam, as my teammate, you can help me with this."

The two worked together to start a cooking fire and get the meal underway. Alex Arlington cooked the fresh catch perfectly, and Adam served the fish on plates, with a side of sliced tomatoes they'd bought at the store in Lewistown.

"Good stuff, Dad," Ashley said, patting her father on the back.

"Time to kiss the cook," Mrs. Arlington said with a smile, leaning over and offering just that to her husband.

Mr. Arlington looked pleased. "I wish I'd had better luck with the fishing part, but you won't taste any sour grapes in my cooking."

After cleaning up the dinner dishes, the family set the lantern on the picnic table and pulled out Mrs. Bear Claw's game box.

"I wonder what these things have to do with anything," Ashley said as she rolled the small wooden figures around in her hands.

"Well, these two are clearly Lewis and Clark, right?" Mr. Arlington asked.

"I'll buy that," Mrs. Arlington answered as the gentle howls and winds of nature could be heard in the background. "But this deer or elk—whatever it is—and this key . . . anybody have any ideas?"

Adam picked up the tiny animal and turned it all around in his hand. He pointed out that the animal figurine had a small hole in the bottom of it. The key matched the hole.

"Check this out," Adam said. He pushed the little wooden key into the keyhole. It didn't open anything or do anything special, but it fit perfectly.

"It clearly connects the key to the elk," Mrs. Arlington observed. "But why?"

"Another mystery," Ashley mused. "But since we've focused mainly on the cards since we've been tracking this thing down, we haven't really given these trinkets a second thought until now."

Mrs. Arlington looked up at the stars and sighed. "The elk and the key," she said. "Hmmm . . ."

"Maybe we'll find out something at the Crow Agency. We leave tomorrow?" Ashley asked.

"Sounds great," her mother said.

The Montana sky seemed to go on forever when the Arlingtons awoke the following morning. The alarm clock chimed in the form of birds chirping Mother Nature's song, and it was a glorious way to be roused. The family got up and went for a brisk walk around the lake with Ashley leading the way.

"Are we camping when we get there?" Ashley asked after breakfast as they began to load the car with gear and supplies.

Her mother proposed staying overnight at a hotel to freshen up and sleep in real beds for a change, and with the plan in place, the family drove off. Still in the heart of Montana but now in the flatland—as opposed to the Rocky Mountain region of Helena, Butte, and West Glacier—Mr. Arlington drove down U.S. 87 all the way to Billings where the family had lunch. Hardin, where the Crow reservation was located, was just a short run down the interstate from there. The Arlingtons checked in at an impressive hotel in Billings.

"We're staying here?" Adam asked, marveling at the large hotel that sported a gym and pool, and a mall with movie theaters across the street.

"I think we all deserve a treat, wouldn't you say?" Mrs. Arlington said, smiling. She put her arms around Adam and Ashley. "You two have traveled so well. And we're especially pleased with the way you've handled yourselves during all the different interactions we've had with people so far."

Mr. and Mrs. Arlington shared a suite, and Ashley and Adam brought their bags into an adjoining suite.

Adam flopped down on one of the queen-sized beds. "Ah, this is living!" he announced happily.

"We could stay here for a month or two," Ashley said to her father with a smile as they gave their approval to the arrangements.

Everyone showered, and then the family went shopping at the mall. After taking in a matinee movie, the Arlingtons worked out together at the spacious hotel gym, which included a basketball court. Of course, they couldn't leave without a game of two-on-two. Ashley was a starter on her high school team, and she and Adam took three out of three games from their parents.

"Okay, this is pathetic," Mr. Arlington said with a sigh, wiping sweat from his brow. "I must be getting old—I'm ready to put my feet up."

"No way, Dad—we haven't even gone for a swim yet!" Adam protested.

"You and your sister can swim if you want, but Dad and I are going to pick up a few newspapers and get caught up on what's happening in the world before dinner," Mrs. Arlington told the kids, rescuing her husband from any further humiliation.

After enjoying the enormous breakfast buffet in the hotel's dining room, the Arlingtons reluctantly checked out the next morning. They headed to Hardin and then south to Crow Agency and Little Bighorn National Monument. The audience sat to watch the reenactment on the grassy hill where Clark had passed about 100 miles to the north seven decades before the fateful battle took place on June 25, 1876.

The Arlingtons saw how hundreds of Sioux and Cheyenne had gathered to resist relocation on the reservation. They watched as Custer divided his forces and moved directly into the midst of the Native American encampment. The sounds of single-shot carbine rifles cracked the air, and multitudes of horses kicked up clouds of dust. Within an hour, Lieutenant Colonel George Armstrong Custer met his legendary end at the hands of the Sioux, led by Crazy Horse and Sitting Bull.

Spectators mobbed Crazy Horse, Custer, and Sitting Bull after the reenactment. The Arlingtons intentionally stayed out of the way for a while. They enjoyed watching the younger children interact with the actors. After Custer had finished signing autographs, the Arlingtons explained their situation. They fully expected him to be as bewildered as the intern at the Great Falls historical society had been. So they were delighted when he immediately knew what they were talking about.

"So, you're the folks I have been holding a mysterious envelope for?" Custer said with a look of relief hidden behind fake blood.

"That's us," Adam said, extending his hand for an introduction. "Custer" introduced himself as Brad Lovejoy.

"You know something, I get here in late May each year, and I don't think I've ever had mail sent to me," Brad said. "I almost tossed the thing right away. But then I recognized the name of the sender, Sarah Bear Claw. She and her family came to the reenactment a few years ago, and we talked for some time after the show."

"About Lewis and Clark?" Adam asked.

"No," Brad explained, "actually we talked about the progress American Indians have made in the century since the time of Little Bighorn, and, sadly, about the many terrible roadblocks they've met along the way. To put it mildly," he added.

Mrs. Arlington nodded. "The oppression of Native Americans has been among our country's greatest disgraces."

The actor jogged over to a trailer and returned with an envelope. As the Arlingtons had come to expect by now, the envelope contained a card and a sheet of paper with some writing about the Lewis and Clark expedition. The card read "5,280, town—and more history."

Ashley pulled out her map in the center of the travel guide she had in her back pocket and quickly decoded the message.

"No doubt on this one," Ashley said. "It's 'Miles City.' And once again, we probably need to talk to the local historical society director."

"You guys are pros!" Brad marveled.

"We've been doing this for a while now," Adam said, recounting the riddles that led to West Glacier, Great Falls, Lewistown, and now the Crow Agency.

"Would you mind if I read this to you, the thing about Lewis and Clark?" Brad Lovejoy asked the Arlingtons. "You can have it after I read it to you, if you want it."

"That would be great," Mr. Arlington said. "If someone had told me last month that Lt. Colonel George Armstrong

Custer would be reading to us about the Lewis and Clark expedition after we watched the Battle of the Little Bighorn . . . well, we wouldn't have come."

"Why not, Dad?" Adam asked.

"Because they would've put me in a hospital, since they'd think I was crazy!" Mr. Arlington answered, drawing laughs from the group.

"Okay," the actor said. "Here goes."

On the Pacific: November 1805 to March 1806

Captain Lewis carried with him a letter of credit signed by Jefferson, guaranteeing payment for the explorers' return by sea via any American or foreign merchant ship encountered in the Columbia River estuary. They saw no ships upon reaching the ocean, nor, as their records reveal, would any enter the turbulent river entrance during their four-month stay at the coast. Actually, the captains never seriously intended to return by sea, preferring instead to establish a camp close to the coast. There they hoped to obtain from trading ships ". . . a fresh supply of Indian trinkets to purchase provisions on our return home."

Due to the absence of game and their unprotected exposure to fierce winter storms on the north shore of the Columbia (Washington State), the party elected to cross the river to the south side (Oregon) where, Indians informed them, elk and deer were numerous. An actual vote of the members was recorded, representing the first American democratically held election west of the Rockies *that included the vote of a woman, Sacagawea, and a black man, York, who was Clark's slave and lifelong companion.*

Crossing the river, they built their 1805-06 winter quarters on a protected site five miles south of modern Astoria, Oregon, naming it Fort Clatsop for their neighbors, the Clatsop Indians. The men spent the winter hunting elk for food and for making clothing and moccasins to replace their worn buckskins. Lewis filled his journal with descriptions of plants, birds, mammals, fish, amphibians, weather data, and much detailed information on Indian cultures. Clark drew illustrations of many of the animals and plants and brought his maps of the journey up to date. Sacagawea joined Clark and a few of the men on a trip to the coast to procure oil and blubber from a "monstrous fish," a whale that had washed up on the beach. On the way, they visited the expedition's salt-making camp at present-day Seaside, Oregon, where several of the men kept a continuous fire burning for nearly a month boiling sea water, to produce twenty gallons of salt. They had reached the Pacific, and it was almost time to return home.

Brad Lovejoy jotted down his name and the number for the school where he was a mathematics teacher during the school year, and the family posed for a picture with him before heading back to the car.

As they headed up the interstate toward Miles City, Ashley flipped through the Montana vacation book that Mrs.

Arlington had ordered earlier in the year when the family was planning the trip. She traced the route Lewis and Clark took on their trip. The explorers entered the state by following the Missouri River from St. Louis into what are the present-day cities of Culbertson and Wolf Point. They continued west through areas that would become the cities of Great Falls and Missoula. On their way back through Montana coming from the west they traveled through present-day Dillon, Three Forks, and finally Miles City before ending their Montana trek through cities now known as Glendive and Sidney.

"We must be almost at the end of our journey," Ashley mused. "The leg of the trip Mr. Lovejoy read about described nearly the end of their journey, before they turned around and headed home, right?"

"Just like we'll be doing soon," her mother said.

Accident!

The drive to Miles City was 118 miles. Like just about everywhere else the Arlingtons had been in Montana, the ride offered gorgeous vistas, and the sunshine and cool breeze refreshed them when they stopped for a picnic lunch.

"We have to move to Montana," Adam declared.

Mr. and Mrs. Arlington just smiled. They could remember their children making similar claims on past vacations in other states. Driving along the Yellowstone River after lunch, the family found a campground just outside Miles City.

"This looks perfect. Let's camp here," Mrs. Arlington said.

"Good idea—it'll give me a chance to even the score on the fishing competition," Mr. Arlington said wryly.

After setting up camp just off the river at the campground, the Arlingtons headed to the Miles City Historical Society and arrived just five minutes before closing time.

"Quite a run of good luck we've had," Mr. Arlington said.

"Cross your fingers, and let's hope we have a little left to end this thing on a high note," Mrs. Arlington said.

"Hello!" Mr. Arlington called out as they entered the building. No one was at the reception area, so Mr. Arlington called out again.

An older gentleman came down the stairs.

"What can I do for you?" asked the man, smiling.

Mr. Arlington introduced his family, and the man told them he was the director of the historical society, Paul Jackson. Mr. Arlington recited the same speech that everyone else in the family had given at one time or another during the trip, and the more he talked, the more Mr. Jackson beamed.

"According to the correspondence I received from Mrs. Bear Claw," the director said, "this is just about the end of the road for your adventure," Jackson said. "I have an envelope back in the safe. Let me get it for you."

Mr. Jackson emerged from a back room with the envelope in his hand.

"According to the part of the correspondence sent to me—which I will gladly show you—this is your final clue in terms of these cards, which I assume you have several of by now," Jackson said. "I met Sarah Bear Claw about fifty years ago. We corresponded once or twice over the years, and when I got this job thirty years ago, I gave her the address in case she wanted to get in touch when we put on a Lewis and Clark expedition show. I never heard from her until a short time ago when this came in the mail.

The postmark was from Butte, and I called out there, but couldn't track her down."

"Unfortunately, we have some bad news about Mrs. Bear Claw," Mrs. Arlington said. "She passed away earlier this week of natural causes."

"God bless that woman's soul," Jackson said. "She was a credit to the Shoshone tribe."

"She was at a relative's home in New Mexico," Mrs. Arlington continued. "Apparently, this mission was important to her."

"She always knew more than she let on—at least that was my feeling," Jackson said, shaking his head of thick white hair. "The time I saw her—and once in her letter to me—she referred vaguely to some information that she said she hadn't shared with anyone. But I couldn't coax it out of her on either occasion. As twenty or thirty years passed, I kind of forgot about it until I received this in the mail." He handed a card to Ashley.

Ashley looked at the card. "This one's different from the others—a longer clue. It says, 'Pompey's Pillar will reveal the object of your quest. Look opposite the signature. What connects the men?'" Ashley looked up and shrugged, then looked at the card again. "It goes on—'Beyond the pillar, the key is in the animal. No more clues. Your quest—a thing as yet unseen even by me, only heard of—ends at Grant-Kohrs, away from everything else in the abandoned cabin.'"

"I don't know about keys and connections, but I can tell you about Pompey's Pillar," Jackson said. "It's on the way back to Billings, about twenty-eight miles east of Billings on Interstate 94. It's a national historic landmark, and Captain William Clark carved his name there on the butte in 1806. It is the only remaining physical evidence along the trail of the Lewis and Clark expedition."

Mr. Jackson handed the sheet of paper that had been included with the card to Mr. Arlington.

"I'll go ahead and read this to everyone," Mr. Arlington said, clearing his throat.

The Return Journey: March 1806 to September 1806

On March 23, 1806, the explorers started back up the Columbia in newly acquired Indian canoes. At the Great Falls of the Columbia they bartered with local Indians for packhorses and set out toward the north shore of the river on foot. Obtaining riding horses from various tribes along the way, the party reached the Nez Perce villages in May.

While camped among the Nez Perce for a month, waiting for the high mountain snows to melt, the captains gave frontier medical treatment to sick and injured Indians in exchange for native foods. The Nez Perce rounded up the expedition's horses that they had cared for over the winter, easing the captains' concern for adequate transportation as the party resumed its eastward travel in early June. Retracing their outbound trail through the Bitterroots, they were turned back by impassable snowdrifts and made their only "retrograde march" of the entire journey. After a week's delay, they started out again and successfully crossed the mountains. On June 30, they arrived at their outbound "Travelers Rest" camp, eleven

miles south of modern Missoula, Montana, where they
enjoyed a welcome rest from their toils.

On July 3, 1806, the party separated. Lewis, with nine
men, rode directly east to the Great Falls of the Missouri.
Then with three men, he traveled north to explore the
Marias River almost to the present Canadian border.
Meanwhile Clark, with the balance of the party, proceeded
southeasterly on horseback, crossing the Rockies through
today's Gibbons Pass. When they returned to the
Jefferson River (now the Beaverhead River in its upper
reach), the submerged canoes were recovered and repaired.

Mr. Arlington looked up from the paper. "I had almost forgotten about those," he mused. Then he went on reading.

Clark placed some men in charge of the canoes while he
and the others continued on with the horses, all following
the river downstream to the Three Forks junction of the
Missouri River.

Here, the group divided. The canoe travelers continued
down the Missouri to White Bear Island where they
recovered their cached equipment and portaged back
around Great Falls. Clark with the remainder rode
easterly to explore the Yellowstone River. It was during
this stage of the journey, while passing through Shoshone
tribal lands Sacagawea remembered from her childhood,
that Clark praised her "great service to me as a pilot." On
July 25, 1806, Clark named an unusual rock formation

on the south bank of the Yellowstone River (Montana)
"Pompy's Tower" in honor of Sacagawea's son.

All of the parties were reunited on August 12 near the
confluence of the Yellowstone and the Missouri rivers.
Here, Clark learned that Lewis had been shot while
searching for game in the brushy shoreline of the
Missouri. In his buckskin clothing the captain was
mistaken for an elk by a hunting companion. Clark
treated and dressed the wound with medicines they carried.
Arriving at the Mandan villages on August 17, the
Charbonneau family was mustered out of the expedition.
The remainder of the party headed down the Missouri on
the last leg of the homeward journey.

"How do you think this will end, Mom?" Adam asked.
"Are we on a search for knowledge, or is there actually
something we can get our hands on when we solve this
mystery?"

"I don't really know what lies ahead, to answer your
question," Mrs. Arlington said. "But I do believe that there
is something, somewhere, that will answer a lot of the
questions you and Ashley—and your father and I—have
thought about."

Mr. Arlington extended a hand to Paul Jackson. "Let's
go ahead and let Mr. Jackson close up shop for the day,"
he said. "Thank you, sir. You've been very helpful."

"Please let me know how this turns out, and please take
some photos or video if you do find something," Jackson
said.

"We'll do that," Mrs. Arlington promised.

The Arlingtons headed back to the campground on the Yellowstone River. Along the way, they stopped for additional supplies and prepared to make the most of the long light of a summer's evening with fishing and dinner.

When they'd set up back at camp, Mr. Arlington was a step ahead of everyone else heading toward the river, eager to get a head start and, he hoped, a fish to end his drought.

"I vow to catch dinner for all of us tonight," he said, brandishing his fishing pole comically.

"I don't know, Alex, these kids are quite the fishermen," Mrs. Arlington said with a laugh.

Mr. Arlington walked toward the river and took a few steps backward as he cast his line. Adam was watching his father and could see his feet were dangerously close to the crumbling edge.

"Watch out, Dad!" Adam screamed.

Adam's warning was of no use. The ground on the bank had broken away beneath Mr. Arlington's weight. He fell ten feet to the riverbed and lay motionless in the water.

Answers

"Alex! Alex!" Mrs. Arlington cried, as she and Ashley jumped down the bank and reached Mr. Arlington before the strong current could carry him off.

"What happened?" Mr. Arlington moaned, suddenly sputtering water from his mouth. "My ankle—I think it's hurt."

Ashley and Adam stood by, feeling helpless, while their mother attended to their father.

Mrs. Arlington thought the ankle looked broken. She asked her husband a few questions to check his mental clarity, and when his answers seemed a little vague she sent Adam for help at the camp hosts' trailer. An ambulance arrived shortly after, and the emergency medical technicians helped Mr. Arlington onto a stretcher, up the riverbank, and into the ambulance. All the while, Mrs.

Arlington held her husband's hand, and Adam and Ashley followed close behind.

Late in the evening, the family clustered around Alex Arlington's hospital bed, trying to be cheerful.

"It's only a couple of days, Ash," her father was saying. Although he managed a small smile, his voice sounded ragged and weary.

"And we'll be right here with you, honey," Mrs. Arlington assured him. The doctor had diagnosed a sprained ankle and a concussion of a nature serious enough that he intended to hold the patient for a few days, until the fatigue and wooziness associated with concussion passed.

A nurse told the family it was time to leave and give Mr. Arlington a chance to rest.

"We'll see you in the morning, Dad," Adam said, mustering a cheerful voice.

His father raised a weak hand. "Listen, everybody," he began. "I love you all, but I don't want to see you in the morning."

The Arlingtons exchanged looks of confusion.

"I mean it. You will be on your way to Pompey's Pillar, as planned." He raised his hand again to quiet his family's protests. "I mean it now. I'm just going to be sleeping this one off for a couple days, and nothing will make me get better faster than if I know you're out there pursuing this thing. Please!" He sighed with the exertion of making his point, and Mrs. Arlington asked her children to wait for her outside the room. When she joined them, she looked tired, but resigned.

"He means it," she said with a shrug. "And he's right. There's really nothing we can do for him here, and it would just make him sick to think we're spending the last couple days of our vacation sitting at his bedside while he snores." She pulled her kids in for a hug, and the three of them stood clinging together in the hall, the events of the evening suddenly making them all feel exhausted.

"I guess the three of us will be on our way to Pompey's Pillar first thing tomorrow morning," Mrs. Arlington said.

Despite the late hour and the upsetting events of the evening, Ashley and Adam couldn't help but smile.

The next morning, after breakfast and a phone call to the hospital to be assured Mr. Arlington was holding steady, the three Arlingtons packed up the campsite in preparation for the drive to Pompey's Pillar.

"I know we'll do just fine with the three of us," Adam said. "But I for one am going to miss Dad's sense of humor; now I'm the only one who's really funny!"

Ashley and her mother rolled their eyes.

"You're the only one who *thinks* you're funny," Ashley said, playfully grabbing hold of Adam.

"No fair," Adam said, wrestling free. "Now it's two women and one man—the odds are against me on any family vote!"

"I'd say 'man' is a stretch, bud," Ashley teased.

"Okay," Mrs. Arlington interrupted, pointing at the map. "Let's get serious and see where we are here."

Ashley walked over to the picnic table where her mother sat and ran her finger along the red and black lines that veined the map.

"Hey," she said slowly. "Check this out—assuming after we stop at Pompey's Pillar we head back to the motor home in Butte—wait, let me start from where we started."

"Ash, what are you blabbing about?" Adam questioned, impatient.

"No, seriously, there's something funny here . . . we started in Butte and went to West Glacier. Then, it was southeast to Great Falls and then to Lewistown. We traveled to Hardin, then the Crow Reservation, and then Miles City, and now we're on our way to Pompey's Pillar near Billings. And then we'll head back to Butte."

Adam rolled his eyes and heaved an exaggerated sigh. "Very good, Ms. Map Skills. What's your point?" he asked.

Ashley stuck out her tongue at her brother.

"Enough, enough," Mrs. Arlington said, laughing. "What have I got, a couple of kindergartners as travel companions?"

"Okay, look. If you imagine curves connecting the dots of the towns, do you see the shape?"

"Hey!" Adam shouted. "It's in the shape of an ampersand, just like on the big paper that came in the game box!"

"Then there really is a rhyme and reason to this madness—at least there appears to be at this point," Mrs. Arlington said with a tone of wonder in her voice. "And it links us back to what we found in the box that we got in Butte. That's a good sign."

Adam got up from the picnic table and doused the campfire over which they'd cooked their breakfast to make sure it was completely out, something his father was in the habit of taking care of. Mrs. Arlington smiled.

Ashley volunteered to drive, and before long they saw signs for Pompey's Pillar, and then the sandstone tower itself, rising from the surrounding landscape.

"What connects the men?" Adam read again from the card, mulling it over as they pulled into the parking area. "Plenty—their expedition, the adventure, the history they made together . . ."

"I know—I don't get it," Ashley said, maneuvering the SUV into a space. "But I'm hoping it'll come clear at the pillar 'opposite the signature,' as the card says."

At the base of the pillar, they were surprised at the height of Clark's signature. The Bureau of Land Management brochure pointed out that in the time since 1806, the rock on which Clark stood to engrave his name had washed away. Earlier petroglyphs carved by American Indians had eroded as well. However, protective screens had been installed as early as 1882 to protect and preserve this evidence of the expedition.

"This is so cool," Adam said. "But where's the clue?"

"If it were directly opposite the signature, it would be about here," Mrs. Arlington said, pointing to a plaque mounted on a rock. Adam moved closer to the plaque, which read across the top:

To Commemorate the Lewis & Clark Expedition

Ashley stepped closer, too. "'What connects the men?' Easy! An ampersand; check it out!" she cried.

Mrs. Arlington froze in her steps. "Good work, Ashley!" she cried, clapping.

"You're right! An ampersand!" Adam proclaimed. "We were just making this one too hard! In all the Lewis and

Clark things we've seen, most have had an ampersand instead of the word 'and' between Lewis and Clark. And like you said, Ash, this whole trip route has taken the shape of an ampersand!" he added, excitedly.

"Curious," Mrs. Arlington murmured. "I'm not sure what this means, or how it leads to the next stop on the journey. But since your father will be in the hospital at least another night, we'll just go ahead to Grant-Kohrs tomorrow, like the last clue instructed," Mrs. Arlington said. "I guess the object of our quest is an ampersand of all things!"

"Right, and the card said, 'the key is in the animal,' whatever that means," Ashley pointed out. "We already had that clue, though; remember how you fit the key into the little wooden elk, Adam?"

"Yeah," her brother said, nodding his head. "We'll just have to wait and see how it all comes together."

The drive to Billings took a half hour. The family—minus one—had lunch there and continued on Interstate 94, getting off at Three Forks and heading toward Cardswell on state route 2. There, between the towns of Three Forks and Cardswell, was the Lewis and Clark Caverns State Park, Montana's first state park. It included highly decorated limestone caverns, and the Arlingtons went on the last tour of the day before heading toward Butte and the motor home.

"It feels good to be 'home' again," Ashley said as they pulled into the campground. "But I sure wish Dad was with us."

"We can call him," Mrs. Arlington said.

"Great!" Adam said, retrieving the cell phone and dialing up his father's room at the hospital.

"Hello," a thin voice said, "this is Alex Arlington."

"This is Adam Arlington—it's me, Dad," Adam said jokingly. "How are you?"

"I could only be better if I was still with you," Mr. Arlington said. "I'm feeling okay—but terribly sleepy. So, don't keep me hanging here, son," Mr. Arlington said. "Tell me what you learned today."

Adam recounted the travels of the day and told his father about the stop at Pompey's Pillar.

"Exciting stuff," Mr. Arlington said. "Boy, I wish I could be there for all of this."

Ashley talked with her father briefly, and while their mother took a turn on the phone, Ashley took out her novel and Adam started to put on his portable CD player.

"Kids," their mother began as soon as she hung up the phone, "I know Dad's not with us here, but I think it might be a good time to think about where we are on this trip, and where we're going. What we've learned, what we can take away from these experiences . . ."

Adam and Ashley rolled their eyes at each other, a look that didn't go unnoticed by their mother.

"Now, I'm serious," she said. "It's important to review things as you go through life."

"We know, we know, Mom," Adam said. "But you always make us 'review' right when we're about to do something else that's more fun!"

"Anything's more fun than 'reviewing,'" Ashley said. But she said it good-naturedly, and she was clearly already resolved to the task. "I think what I've been learning the most is that it's about perseverance," she began. "This has all been really fun—but we've had disappointments along the way, and setbacks, and sometimes I kind of wanted just to go hike in Glacier, like we'd planned, instead of driving around all over the state on somebody else's mission. But what if we'd given up? We'd be the ones missing out. And in the end, we might be doing something really special, who knows?"

"You're so right, Ash," her mother agreed. "Perseverance is the same thing that keeps *you* on top of your basketball game and Lewis and Clark on the trail of adventure and discovery."

"Yeah, but we're talking levels here, Mom," Adam said. The three shared a laugh.

"Well, how about you, Adam?" his mother prompted.

"I think I have learned as much on this trip as I have on any," Adam said. "It seems like this whole riddle-game has been about not losing sight of the big picture—and at the same time, not forgetting the value of every little step."

"Go on," said Mrs. Arlington.

"Every little clue has been like a link in the chain— and if one link is weak, the chain snaps. It's like at cross-country practice—sometimes I'm so sick of the drills and interval training and speed work. But I know those things are links in the chain. I can't enjoy that feeling I get at the end of a race if I haven't done all the work that led to crossing the finish line. And I couldn't cross the finish line without teammates and coaching and training . . . you know what I mean?"

"Yeah, honey, I know what you mean," Mrs. Arlington said, putting an arm around her son. "And the links in this chain have been our family to Mrs. Bear Claw and everyone at all the places we've been so far," she said. "If even one person had pulled out of the process—by not passing along a note or by throwing it away—any of those things could have cut the mission short. There is a sense of responsibility that comes with any joint venture. The people we've met here have all seemed to sense that there was a big picture somewhere and that they were all links in a chain."

Discovery!

The drive north the next morning from Butte to Grant-Kohrs National Historic Site took only about forty minutes. Despite the distractions of mountain ranges on both sides and peaceful meadowlands near the historic mining town of Deer Lodge, Adam and Ashley couldn't wait to get to the Grant-Kohrs Ranch at the north end of town.

"What do you think this ampersand is—I mean, do you think it's a drawing or carved from stones?" Adam asked his mother and Ashley.

"I don't know. I wouldn't think it's made from rubies or diamonds or anything like that," Mrs. Arlington said. "Maybe it's carved from the wood like the figurines that came in the box."

"I don't know," Ashley added. "I still don't really understand the meaning of it all. I mean—an ampersand? Yeah, it connects the men, like the clue card asked. But there must be more to it. I'd hate to think we crisscrossed the state in search of a grammatical sign!"

Grant-Kohrs turned out to be a historic treasure. It was the headquarters for an 1800s cattle empire that grazed cattle in four states and in Canada. Still standing were the bunkhouse, a blacksmith shop, and a wagon collection. Adam and Ashley recognized the huge ranch house from pictures in the travel guide.

"Good morning," an elderly woman said at the entrance. "Are you here for the day?"

"Well, we're not really sure," Mrs. Arlington said. "Is there a director here?"

"A director?" the woman said. "Jim Thomas, from the National Park Service, he runs things here. If it's really important, I guess I could page him for you. They're doing a lot of work today, getting rid of some old buildings that are beyond restoration."

"Like what?" Adam said.

"Oh, there are some old outbuildings that have become a safety hazard—nothing that endangers folks touring the ranch area here, though, just an abandoned cabin," she said.

"Oh, no! They've got to stop the demolition!" Adam shouted, jumping up and down.

The woman was completely taken aback.

"Please, ma'am," said Mrs. Arlington, stepping in and putting a calming hand on her son's shoulder. "We have some important and credible information that leads us to believe there's an abandoned cabin here on the property that is of considerable value."

The woman still looked nothing but skeptical.

"If we could just speak with the person in charge, I'm sure we can straighten this out—it's very important." Mrs. Arlington looked quietly into the woman's eyes. "I simply have to ask you to take a leap of faith," she said, imploring her to help them.

The woman hesitated but seemed to let in a chink of doubt. "I can page Jim, if you folks think it's that important," the woman said, finally. "But I don't have any way to get in touch with the crew knocking down the cabin and hauling the wood away. They're on the other side of the property."

Before long, a tall man rode up on a horse and hopped off outside the entryway. The woman introduced him as Jim Thomas, the proprietor of the property.

"I understand there's some problem with the demo?" Jim Thomas began, looking confused.

Mrs. Arlington introduced herself and her children, and explained the situation as clearly and quickly as she could. At the mention of Mrs. Bear Claw, Thomas interrupted.

"Is this a 'Sarah' Bear Claw we're talking about?" he asked.

"Yes, that's right," Mrs. Arlington nodded. "Do you know her?"

"Well, I don't know the woman herself, but I do know the name because we received an envelope from her last week with instructions to keep it for the people who came asking for it."

"Do you still have the envelope?" Ashley eagerly asked.

"Yes, I believe it's still in my office," Thomas responded. "I assume you'd like to see it?"

Before Ashley could respond, Adam quickly interjected, "Yes, we would, Mr. Thomas, but what about the demolition? You can't let them tear down that cabin!"

"Are you folks sure that old cabin is part of your puzzle?" Thomas asked, still confused about how the cabin fit into the picture.

"Is the cabin you are knocking down today the only abandoned one on the property?" Mrs. Arlington asked.

"It sure is," Thomas said. "We've been very careful to restore everything possible. But that ol' cabin has outlived its usefulness, and we can't do much with it. You really sure you got the right cabin in mind? The place is a real dump, if you'll excuse my saying so."

"We need to see it. Please," Mrs. Arlington said.

Jim Thomas seemed to relent a little. "It's a rough road there," Thomas said. "It's just a wagon road—I could get you all horses . . ."

"Come on, get in, and we'll go there in four-wheel drive," Mrs. Arlington suggested. "We're trying to save history here!"

"Okay," Thomas said. "Let's get to it. We'll stop at my office on the way so I can grab that envelope for you. They just got the equipment out to the demolition site, so I'd reckon they're just getting started. But it won't take long once they start."

Mrs. Arlington put the SUV in four-wheel drive and followed Thomas's directions to his office. After a quick stop they continued along a rugged path. It wasn't even a dirt road, just a couple of wheel ruts with deep grass between them.

"Over the years this road has only been used by a couple of trucks we use to run the cattle herds," Thomas said, his voice bouncing as the vehicle handled the rough road.

"You know what's odd about this," he went on, "one time back in the early 1800s, Captain Meriwether Lewis visited here, according to our records. It was just a short visit—he'd just been named Governor of Upper Louisiana Territory."

"Wow!" Adam said. "I can't wait to find out what this is all about!"

"Me, too," Ashley said. "This is more than we could ever have hoped for."

Ashley showed Thomas the card they'd been given in Miles City.

"Here's the part about this ranch," Ashley said, pointing to a line on the card.

"'The key is in the animal,'" Thomas read. "'Your quest ends at Grant-Kohrs, away from everything else in the abandoned cabin.'"

"Does that make sense?" Adam asked.

"Not a bit," Thomas said. "But I can tell you that to the best of my knowledge, that's the only abandoned cabin we've had that wasn't planned for restoration. As far as a key being in the animal . . . there were no keys to enter the cabin. And I can tell you there certainly aren't any animals housed in there."

"That must be it!" Ashley said as Mrs. Arlington steered the vehicle toward a clearing.

"Honk your horn!" Jim Thomas said to Mrs. Arlington. "Smitty's on the bulldozer, and as soon as he gets it into gear, whatever history you are looking for ain't gonna be there!"

No sooner had she stopped the SUV than Jim Thomas opened his door and jumped out, waving his arms. The man called Smitty killed the bulldozer motor and jumped down to the ground.

"What's up, Jim?" he asked, puzzled.

"Well, I'm not real sure," Jim Thomas answered. "But these folks think there might be something inside this cabin that has some sort of historical significance."

"Jim, we've been over this a million times," Smitty said. "The only thing in this building is some old wood and enough dust mites to start a colony."

"I don't doubt it," Thomas said. "But let's go ahead and give them a few minutes to look inside, just to be on the safe side."

"You're the boss," Smitty said, crossing his arms across his chest. "You can pay me to do my work, or you can pay me to stand around."

Jim Thomas carefully opened the door of the cabin, making sure the wall would not fall on the Arlingtons—or anyone else. The sunlight was streaming into the cabin from two windows and a good-sized hole on the roof.

"See?" Smitty said gruffly. "All that thing has is a couple of jars, a few tattered rugs—if you can call them that—and a rotting elk head on the wall."

"An elk head?" Adam asked, looking up at the wall. High on the wall, just under where the wall met the ceiling, was a mounted elk head.

"That thing must be almost a hundred years old," Thomas said. "It's ratty as all get-out, not worth the time to salvage it."

"The elk," Ashley said. "The key fit in the elk, remember?"

"That's what I was thinking," Adam said.

Mrs. Arlington pulled the wooden figurines from her pocket and showed them to Thomas and Smitty.

"'The key is in the animal,'—that's what the card said, right?" asked Thomas.

"Yeah—we're guessing that any answer we're going to find is up there," Adam said, pointing toward the elk head. "Can we get it down?"

Smitty and Thomas brought in a ladder and climbed up to the animal head. The elk head came down with minimal resistance to Thomas's screwdriver. Back on the ground, Thomas separated the stuffed head from its mounting block.

"Here you go," he said to Adam. "Or do you want me to do the looking?"

"I'll do it, if that's all right," Adam said.

"You'd better borrow my gloves," Smitty said, a little grudgingly, but obviously as curious as the rest of them, now.

Adam put the gloves on and fished out a bunch of stuffing from the elk's head. "I feel something!" he said, his arm so far into the head that only his elbow could be seen. "Oh, man, it's heavy!"

He pulled out a large wooden box about ten inches long and five inches wide.

"That's the same wood as the figurines!" Ashley said, holding them up and comparing them to the box.

"The box is sealed," Smitty noted, pointing to the wax that covered the crease of the box. "This thing is airtight and watertight. So, if there is something inside it, it shouldn't be damaged."

Ashley helped Adam as they used the screwdriver to carefully break the seal and open the box. A small piece of paper fell out.

"I am a woman of limited means," the note read, "and I have little contact with people I could trust to care for this treasure. I am with child, and if I have a girl, I will give her the middle name of the one-time owner of this treasure, Sacagawea. Please take care of this, and do the right thing."

The Connection

"I can't believe it!" Ashley said. "This must be Mrs. Bear Claw's mother! It must have been passed down to her by a relative, and then she must have hidden it here in the early 1900s. Why would she have hidden it here?"

"She must have seen a lot of things in her life. It was probably a tough life, and we may never know the details," Mrs. Arlington said. "For whatever reason, she trusted that in time, whoever found this legacy would take care of it."

"Mrs. Bear Claw herself never even saw this—remember? The last clue said it was 'unseen even by me,'" Adam reminded them.

"Let's find out what it is," Ashley said. A leather bag lay in the box with a letter tucked alongside. Adam carefully opened the letter.

"The date on it looks like 1809," Adam said.

"My good friend William Clark," Ashley read. She glanced up, a look of shock in her eyes, then went on.

Ours was a journey of purpose and mission. We covered more miles in our years together than most will in a lifetime. When I was back in Washington, I received a pair of newspaper clippings in the U.S. Mail about our expedition. In both headlines, instead of stating Lewis and Clark, we were abbreviated as Lewis & Clark. In future stories, the ampersand was used, and it remained in the back reaches of my mind. After I was appointed Governor of the Louisiana Territory, I visited Grant-Kohrs outside of Deer Lodge, just taking a final look at the grand land you and I had traversed only a year earlier. There is a blacksmith shop here on Grant-Kohrs among the mammoth cattle operation. While at Grant-Kohrs, I commissioned a blacksmith, who had just come over from England, to create this special gift from me to you, commemorating our voyage. This cast iron ampersand stands out little to the common eye. But in view of what we experienced together, I feel it is a solid memento. We are intertwined by the ampersand in newspapers everywhere. While I assume you will not soon forget me, I want you to have this to post on the wall of your home or office. It is a small gesture but a huge reminder of the most exciting time in my life. Our voyage was not without trials or tribulations, often on a seemingly daily basis. Yet, a day does not pass where I do not hear about the historical and logistical value of our expedition—some even think it might one day be in history books! Another said our route might one day be commemorated on a world map! While I find it foolhardy to believe that anyone would put my name in a book that will last through the ages, I know this cast-iron ampersand can be a testimonial to all we accomplished and to how much I appreciate your courage, wisdom, and heart. Surely, our route will be retraced in the future. But I cannot imagine ever again meeting someone who influenced my life the way you have. The going is rough for me now, as you might have heard. I long for the days of the western sunset and the constant excitement that coursed through my veins waking up in mountains or prairie. You are a man before his time, yet you are a man for the ages.

Godspeed to you,
Meriwether Lewis

"Wow!" Ashley said. "Lewis must have died soon after he sent this to Clark. Who would have thought . . ."

"Say, we almost forgot about the envelope, Ash. Do you think there is more of their journey inside?" Adam chimed in, once again intrigued by the explorers' exciting voyage.

"That's exactly what it is, Adam," Ashley said with a smile as she opened the envelope. "Listen to this."

After September 23, 1806

On September 23, 1806, the tattered Corps of Discovery arrived at St. Louis and "received a hearty welcome from its inhabitants." It had been a great expedition. Jefferson's explorers had covered 8,000 miles of territory over a period of two years, four months, and nine days. Their records contributed important new information concerning the land, its natural resources, and its native peoples. Lewis and Clark learned that the surprising width of the Rocky Mountain chain effectively destroyed Jefferson's hoped-for easy connection between the Missouri and Columbia River systems. This finding was the expedition's single most important geographical discovery, resulting in a route over South Pass (Wyoming) during later follow-up trips westward by fur traders and other explorers. There had been plenty of difficulties, but Lewis and Clark were as firm friends as when they started. Congress rewarded the officers and men of the military enterprise, including Toussaint Charbonneau, with grants of land. Sacagawea received no compensation for her services.

On February 28, 1807, President Jefferson picked Lewis to be Governor of Upper Louisiana Territory. His career started well, but controversy involving government finances arose in 1809 culminating with his decision to travel to Washington, D.C., to resolve the dispute. Traveling through Tennessee, on October 11, 1809, Governor Meriwether Lewis died mysteriously from gunshot wounds inflicted while at Grinder's Stand, a public roadhouse. It is not *known conclusively whether he was murdered or committed suicide. His grave lies where he died, within today's Natchez Trace National Parkway near Hohenwald, Tennessee.*

"That's what you told us the first day of our trip, Mom," Adam interrupted. "Sorry, Ash, you can keep reading."

Clark enjoyed a lifelong, honorable career of public service in St. Louis. On March 12, 1807, Jefferson commissioned him Brigadier General of Militia and Indian Agent for Upper Louisiana Territory. In 1813 he was appointed Governor of Missouri Territory, a position he held until Missouri Statehood in 1820. In 1822 he was appointed Superintendent of Indian Affairs by President Monroe. He was reappointed to this post by each succeeding president and served in this capacity for the remainder of his life. Admired by many Indians as their friend and tribal protector, General William Clark died of natural causes in St. Louis, September 1, 1838. He is buried in the Clark family plot at Bellefontaine Cemetery, St. Louis.

On a final, small scrap of paper was a short note. Adam opened it and began to read.

"Check this out!" Adam proclaimed. "It's from William Clark to . . . to . . . Sacagawea!

"Dear Sacagawea," he read, "our faithful friend and valuable expedition member. It has been brought to my attention that you did not receive compensation for your efforts and hard work. You gave part of your life—and soul—to help the U.S. Government during our mission. I have included $400 in this. Should it not be here, contact me immediately, and I will deal with the Pony Express as to what happened to the money. Also included is a special trinket that Meriwether Lewis made to commemorate our mission. As you might have heard, Lewis was killed recently by a gunshot. I cannot look at this memento any longer, yet it is a part of history, and it must be preserved. Please accept this as a token of the appreciation that both I—and the late Meriwether Lewis—hold for you and will always hold for you. I am worried about the direction the U.S. Government is taking with the Indian people. I hope this will change during your lifetime. Please accept this package with my heartfelt prayers and thoughts for you, your family, and your people. May the Great Spirit be with you, the Shoshones, and Indian people everywhere in the West."

"Okay," Mrs. Arlington said. "Now, open the big pouch."

Adam carefully untied the big leather pouch—the heavy one. He undid the last piece of thread and pulled out a cast-iron ampersand.

"Spectacular!" Thomas proclaimed.

"This is history," Smitty added. "We are watching history unfold in front of our eyes. I can't believe it."

"Your hard work has paid off," Thomas said, as Adam passed the ampersand to Ashley and then to Mrs. Arlington, who carefully placed it in Thomas's hands. "Your quest is over."

"No, it isn't," Ashley said. "Not yet."

History in the Making

Ashley again took the ampersand, holding it in the light and blowing some more dust off it. The sunlight caught the dust, casting a special shade of light on a special moment.

"We have to make sure we do everything the way it needs to be done," Ashley said.

"Well, this was found on the Grant-Kohrs property, so I would guess that it probably belongs here," Mrs. Arlington said.

"I think we'd respect whatever you folks decide," Thomas said. "After all, this piece of history would be headed for the dump right now if you hadn't come along and stopped us."

"I have an idea," Ashley said.

"Let's hear it," Thomas said.

"We should display the ampersand here at Grant-Kohrs—at the very blacksmith shop where it was made," Ashley said. "We could put it in a display case with the letter."

Everyone nodded in agreement.

"Good idea," Thomas said.

"Yeah," Adam agreed. "And how about we display each clue where we found it—the one letter in Miles City, the clue from Pompey's Pillar," Adam said. "We could do the same thing in Great Falls and Lewistown, and even at West Glacier. At each spot, we could have a small-scale replica of the cast-iron ampersand. And we could have maps showing the journey Mrs. Bear Claw led us on."

"That's great!" exclaimed Jim Thomas. "Let me make some calls. We'll get the folks you met from Miles City, Great Falls, and everywhere else down here, and we'll have a press conference to announce the memorial. Shoot, we could get a nice display case in place and have someone in our blacksmith shop put together a plaque to commemorate it."

Adam and Ashley looked at each other in silence.

"What is it?" Jim Thomas asked.

"Oh, I think we're just a little sorry we'll have to miss all the excitement," Mrs. Arlington said, speaking for her children. "We're leaving Montana day after tomorrow."

"Well in that case—time's a-wasting." Jim exclaimed. "I've got to get on the horn and pull this thing together for tomorrow."

"All right!" Ashley said. "That would be perfect!"

"Why don't you folks go ahead and take the ampersand with you tonight," Thomas said. "Since you've been kind enough to find it and donate it as a historical marker, you should at least get an evening to study it and talk about it. I'd just like to put it in the clay really quick here and get a molding, if you don't mind."

Ashley handed it to Thomas, and he pressed it into some clay that he had pulled off the front of the bulldozer. He carefully wiped the ampersand off and handed it back to Ashley.

"Then we'll be here tomorrow morning," Mrs. Arlington said. "How does 11:00 A.M. sound?"

"Let's go with high noon," Thomas said. "I'll go back to my office and call the TV stations, newspapers, and radio stations. I'll try and get all the folks you met on this trek down here as well, but I'd imagine we'll be a few short. But I'll do my best. Why don't you good people find a few words to say during the dedication."

"Noon tomorrow," Mrs. Arlington called out as they drove away down the wagon path.

"This is absolutely thrilling!" Mrs. Arlington announced. "I just wish your father could have been here with us today." A look of concern passed across her face. She shook it off. "Listen," she said, "I want one of you to take the lead and speak tomorrow. You can work on the speech together while we eat lunch."

"I think it should be Adam," Ashley said. "Because if he hadn't left the games back home, we wouldn't have asked for games that first night at the convenience store in Butte."

"Sounds like a plan," Mrs. Arlington said. "Just thinking about that makes me realize how unlikely it is that this whole thing unfolded. What a great story."

Mrs. Arlington and the kids were pretty tired when they got back to the motor home that evening. They'd called the hospital on their way back to the motor home and had related the day's fantastic events to Mr. Arlington. After Adam and Ashley had finished talking with their father, Mrs. Arlington spoke with her husband a few minutes alone.

They started packing for a while and then took a break to barbecue burgers and hot dogs. After eating more than they thought they could, Adam and Ashley still wanted to roast marshmallows.

"You two can be the night owls," Mrs. Arlington said, giving each a kiss on the cheek.

"Good night, Mom," Ashley said.

"Love you," Adam added.

"I know your father isn't here right now," Mrs. Arlington said. "But I can say that he and I are both very proud of you two."

Mrs. Arlington retired to the back of the motor home.

"I have some more ideas for our speech," Ashley said.

"I do, too," said Adam.

The brother and sister team spent nearly three hours sitting underneath the motor home's awning as the stars sparkled in the wide-open Montana sky. The morning sun came early to Adam and Ashley, who had stayed up well past midnight. Still, with the noon ceremony on that day's docket and the beginning of the trip home to the East Coast, Adam and Ashley were eager to get a start on the day, and hopped right out of bed when their mother's alarm clock went off at 7:00 A.M.

After a spirited run and a hearty breakfast, the Arlingtons spent more time packing and cleaning in the motor home, then showered and dressed for the ceremony. Once everyone was ready, Ashley drove the SUV toward the Grant-Kohrs National Historical Site. Mrs. Arlington, riding in the backseat, looked at her watch.

"It's about thirty-six miles to Deer Lodge," Mrs. Arlington said. "So, we'll get there a little early, as usual—probably about fifteen to twenty minutes."

After exiting Interstate 90, Grant-Kohrs was soon visible in the distance. The Arlingtons were surprised at the size of the crowd that had gathered. They saw several photographers and even a pair of television news vans with satellite dishes on top.

"Maybe they're going to broadcast live!" Ashley said. "Are you nervous, Adam?"

"A little," Adam admitted. "I'm just trying to keep everything in perspective, like Mom and Dad always tell us to. But it's just hard to believe that nearly two hundred years ago, one of the most famous explorers in American history owned this thing in my hands. I just can hardly believe it."

As soon as they parked the car, Jim Thomas greeted the Arlingtons.

"Come on up here with me, gang," Thomas said. He led them to a podium and stopped to place the ampersand in a large, beautiful fiberglass case with an oak wood base. There were several other smaller versions of the large case. Each one had a small ampersand that looked exactly like the one the Arlingtons had found the day before.

"That's amazing," Adam said to his mother and sister. "And all they had to go from was that quick mold Mr. Thomas made yesterday!"

Thomas turned to Ashley.

"Do you have everything else, Ashley?" Thomas asked.

"Right here," Ashley said, pulling out a folder with the letters and a plastic bag that held the little wooden figurines.

"Let's go ahead and load each display case," Thomas said. "I had my staff carve the name of each town in the respective cases."

"Looks perfect," Mrs. Arlington whispered to Thomas. "It's spectacular."

"Considering we put all of this together in twenty-four hours," he remarked, "I have to say I'm pretty proud of the work, too. Some of the staff and I had coffee on the fire until almost sun-up finishing everything in time."

Thomas smiled broadly as he stepped up to the podium to welcome everyone before explaining the displays that were about to be filled and turning to invite the Arlingtons to help.

Ashley and Adam stepped over to Thomas and were shocked—and very delighted—to see Ranger Kinnison from West Glacier step up to the group. She helped them put the first clues and the "board game" itself, along with the figurines, into the display case marked "Left Iceberg—West Glacier."

Again, a smile crossed Ashley's and Adam's faces as they saw Karen Simon, the director at the Great Falls Historical Society, who helped arrange that case.

"A big trip and a big reward for all of us in the state of Montana," Mrs. Simon said to Ashley and Adam.

Cathy, the clerk from the Trading Post in Lewistown wore a sky-wide smile when she stepped onto the dais.

"Martha Miller wanted to be here," Cathy said, "but her charter finally got off the ground, and she's in Hawaii."

"Thank you so much for coming down today in her place!" Mrs. Arlington said, giving Cathy a hug.

"Next," Thomas said, "is the Miles City case. Unfortunately, it appears Mr. Paul Jackson from the Miles City Historical Society is not able to be here . . ."

"Wait a minute," a voice called from the back of the crowd. "Better late than never!"

Paul Jackson showed his enthusiasm by bounding up on the podium, skipping a step on the way up.

"You kids really did it, didn't you," he said, putting his left arm around Ashley and his right arm around Adam.

"Yes, sir, but not without your help," Ashley said before she turned to help Mr. Thomas load the case.

"Here you go, Mr. Jackson," Thomas said, handing the case to Jackson. "We'll help you with it when we leave."

"Hey, I'm on cloud nine, here, and this just added about ten years to my life. I'll carry it over my shoulder just as I did my pack in World War II!"

"All right, Mr. Jackson," Thomas said with a smile. "And thanks for driving all the way here. It must have taken all night."

"I left as soon as you called yesterday, stayed with relatives about halfway here, and made the rest of the trip this morning," said Jackson, who traveled as far as anyone to be at the ceremony. "I haven't driven this much in years, and it really gave me an emotional boost just to see the state again, especially at dusk last night and then again at sunrise this morning."

Adam and Ashley felt a momentary letdown when they found out no representative from the Little Bighorn Battlefield was able to make it to Grant-Kohrs. But Jackson gladly volunteered to deliver that display case on his way home.

"I haven't been down that direction in twenty-five years," Jackson said. "I'll be more than happy to take care of it."

The last of the cases was bound for Pompey's Pillar. "I can take care of that one," a voice hollered from the crowd.

"Dad!"

Trail's End

There were a few moments of confusion as Mr. Arlington made his way up to the podium. The ceremony was interrupted, only briefly, for a family hug, during which Mr. Arlington whispered to his children's questions, "I'll tell you later."

"Let's finish off this big one," Thomas said to Ashley, who was helping him, "and then we'll perch it right here in front of this makeshift stage. We'll move the display out to where the old cabin is this afternoon."

"Old cabin?" Adam said, his attention piqued by Thomas's words. "That thing was torn down yesterday, right?"

"No way," Thomas said. "It is beyond restoring, we know that. But we remounted the walls, so while folks can't go inside it, they can certainly look in the windows. Out front, next to this case with the cast-iron ampersand, we are going to put the elk's head on the side of the building in a mounted fiberglass case."

"That'll be quite the display," Mrs. Arlington said.

"We expect that everyone will be pretty proud of it," Thomas said. "And, of course, we are pretty grateful to you all for making this happen."

With all of the display cases now filled, Thomas stepped back to the microphone to address the crowd again.

"Thanks to all of our friends and the media for being here today," Thomas said. "As I wrote in the press release we sent out last night, we're here for a very special occasion. A piece of history was unearthed yesterday here on the ranch by a couple of kids whose ages belie their maturity. They happened upon a couple of clues in an old box in Butte. They traveled the state in a pattern that would soon be discovered to be an ampersand and ended up stopping me and my men from tearing down an old cabin here on the property last night. They uncovered this cast-iron piece of history and a couple of notes and letters that had been hidden in a stuffed elk's head that was mounted on the cabin's wall. Folks, this has sat on the property for close to a hundred years. I think it says a lot about the Lewis and Clark spirit these kids, Ashley and Adam Arlington, displayed to make this day happen."

Pulling out a pack from a shelf on the podium, he removed four small black cast-iron ampersands. "These are for the Arlington family," he said. "We will also reproduce ampersands one-half as big as these to be sold at all historical and tourist sites across the state—and for that we must also thank the Arlingtons. So, without anything further, please welcome our distinguished guests, Anne, Adam, Ashley, and—"

"Alex," the family provided.

"—and Alex Arlington."

The thirty or so people stood and clapped. Ashley stood next to Adam, and he pulled out the words he and his sister had put down on paper.

"Before I get to this," Adam said, holding up the paper, "I'd just like to thank everyone for their kindness. We have been treated really well in Montana, and we're very lucky to have made so many good friends in such a short time."

Ashley smiled and waved, returning to her seat next to Mrs. Arlington. Adam cleared his throat and looked into the crowd with the Montana landscape as a backdrop and a sea of blue sky above him.

"What we have experienced here in Montana has sure been a once-in-a-lifetime vacation for us!" he began. "To be honest, sometimes we wondered what we were doing, whether we were in Glacier Park or on the highway bound for Miles City or Great Falls. We kept thinking, 'How can this amount to anything? What are we doing?' There were some stops where we almost missed a clue or a person we were supposed to contact. But you know, even if we had missed a clue or if we hadn't been able to finish Mrs. Bear Claw's journey, we would still have to think of this as a victory—because we were able to make friends along the way. I also think that we've had a little glimpse of how Lewis and Clark felt on their journey—wondering what lies ahead, why are we here, is there any end in sight—those kinds of questions. Although I know we're talking 'levels' here." Adam smiled at Ashley then, before continuing.

"Those on the expedition had to experience feelings of self-doubt on a daily basis. What did they do about it? They moved forward. They knew that only the future—and the frontier—held the keys to what they were looking for. They also met strangers, just like we did, at every turn. They hoped and prayed for positive encounters because in their era an introduction could be fatal if things didn't go well. Lewis and Clark told us a lot through their expedition, and not just from the exploration itself or the maps that came out of it. They taught us about courage and about having a vision."

Applause came from the audience. Adam folded up the paper, but he wasn't through speaking.

"My sister and I had an idea, even though we might be out of line here," he said. He looked over at Jim Thomas, who encouraged him with a nod.

"We know that Sacagawea was never compensated by the U.S. Government for her help to the expedition," Adam said. "And it doesn't seem as though they could have made it without her, does it? So, I'd like to ask if a certain amount from the sale of these ampersand souvenirs could be donated to a Native American cause, maybe a college fund?"

Everyone in the audience gave Adam a standing ovation as he went to sit down. Jim Thomas walked back to the podium.

"I eagerly embrace Ashley and Adam's suggestion, and what do you say we donate 50 percent of the ampersand profits to a Native American college fund? Plus, on behalf of Grant-Kohrs, I'd like to donate $1,000 to that to-be-determined fund right now."

"I'm in for $500," said Mr. Jackson.

"I'll chip in $250," said a woman in the audience.

"Count on $300 from me," said another man in a cowboy hat in the back of the crowd. Other voices shouted their promised donations.

"All right!" Thomas said ecstatically. "That's the spirit of the west that we appreciate! Thanks to everyone for being here. We'll have a reception up at the ranch house to feed and water all of you before you hit the road home. God bless you all!"

"I still can't believe you made it in time for the ceremony, Dad," Ashley told her father later that evening when the family was resting back at the motor home in Butte.

"I took the bus to a car rental place the second I was discharged," Mr. Arlington said. "My ankle doesn't keep me from driving an automatic, so Mom and I decided that would be the easiest way to get me from there to here. I just prayed I'd be here to share the moment with you."

Their mother smiled and nodded. "Last night on the phone we agreed to keep Dad's arrival a little bit of a surprise for you two. Didn't it all work out perfectly?"

The next morning, after dropping off the display case and ampersand with the Bureau of Land Management Office at Pompey's Pillar, the family, for a final time, passed over the Yellowstone River—the river that Mr. Arlington had fallen into.

"You know, since it's obvious you are going to be all right," Mrs. Arlington said, "it's too bad we didn't have the video camera going. I bet you we could have won some good money on one of those amazing video television shows . . . I can hear the host of the show now, 'See this guy; he thinks he's going fishing—but he decides to forget about using a pole. He's going to catch a fish with his teeth!'"

Everyone got a laugh out of that one, even Mr. Arlington.

"That's it—rub a little salt in the wound, like I'm not hurt enough already," Mr. Arlington joked. "I'm down to one good ankle and a headache; let me keep my pride!"

"I'm sorry, honey—we did have a rough go of things for a while there, didn't we?" Mrs. Arlington admitted.

"We sure did," Ashley agreed. "But seriously, that's what it's all about, isn't it? I mean, if there's one thing I'll take away from this journey it's this: It's all about moving on, about persevering and following through, whether things are easy or you hit a rough patch."

The family rode on in silence for a few moments, remembering Captains Lewis and Clark, Sacagawea, Mrs. Bear Claw, and all the people who'd been a part of this journey.

Adam smiled. "It's like Captain Lewis said, right?" he began. "'Good or bad, we must make the portage.'"

Montana

Fun
Fact
Files

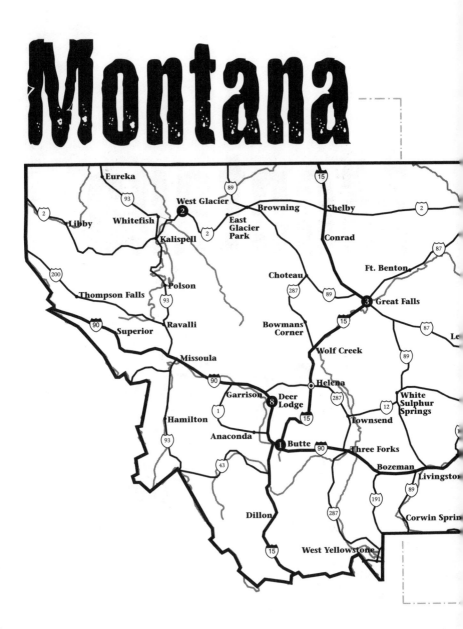

Montana

Eureka

West Glacier ●②

Libby

Whitefish

Kalispell

East Glacier Park

Browning

Shelby

Choteau

Conrad

Ft. Benton

Thompson Falls

Polson

Ravalli

Superior

Bowmans Corner

Wolf Creek

Great Falls ●③

Missoula

Helena

Garrison

Deer Lodge ●⑧

White Sulphur Springs

Townsend

Hamilton

Anaconda

●❶ Butte

Three Forks

Bozeman

Livingston

Dillon

Corwin Spring

West Yellowstone

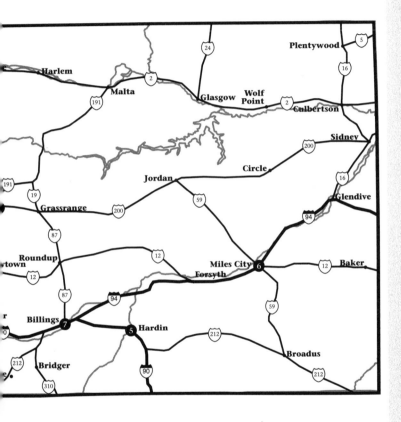

The Arlingtons' Route

1. Butte
2. West Glacier
3. Great Falls
4. Lewistown

5. Hardin
6. Miles City
7. Billings
8. Deer Lodge

Names and Symbols

Origin of Name:

Chosen by J. M. Ashley, *montana* is a Latinized Spanish word meaning "mountainous."

Nicknames:

Big Sky Country, Bonanza State, Treasure State, Land of Shining Mountains

Motto:

Oro y Plata—"Gold and Silver"

State Symbols:

flower—bitterroot
tree—ponderosa pine
stones—sapphire and Montana agate
bird—western meadowlark
animal—grizzly bear
fish—cutthroat trout

Geography

Location:

Northern Great Plains/Rocky Mountains
sometimes considered part of the Pacific Northwest

Borders:

Canada—British Columbia, Alberta, and Saskatchewan (north)
North and South Dakota (east)
Wyoming (south)
Idaho (west)

Area:

147,047 square miles (4th largest state)

Highest Elevation:

Granite Peak, Park County (12,799 feet)

Lowest Elevation:

Kootenai River, Lincoln County (1,800 feet)

Nature

National Parks:

Glacier National Park
Yellowstone National Park (partial)

National Forests:

Beaverhead-Deerlodge National Forest
Bitterroot National Forest
Custer National Forest
Flathead National Forest
Gallatin National Forest
Helena National Forest
Kootenai National Forest
Lewis and Clark National Forest
Lolo National Forest

Weather

The hottest temperature ever recorded in Montana was 117 degrees, recorded at Glendive on July 20, 1893, and again at Medicine Lake on July 5, 1937. On January 20, 1954, Montana set a cold record for the lower 48 states, recording a temperature of 70 degrees below zero at Rogers Pass, north of Helena.

Montana also set a world record for the greatest temperature change in twenty-four hours on January 23, 1916. On that day residents of Browning saw the temperature plummet exactly 100 degrees, from 44 degrees *above* zero to 56 degrees *below* zero!

People and Cities

Population:

880,000 (1998 census)
799,000 (1990 census)

Capital:

Helena

Ten Largest Cities (as of 1998):

Billings (91,195)
Great Falls (57,758)
Missoula (51,204)
Butte–Silver Bow (34,051)
Bozeman (28,522)
Helena (27,982)
Kalispell (15,678)
Havre (10,232)
Anaconda–Deer Lodge County (10,093)
Miles City (8,882)

Counties:

56 (plus a small part of Yellowstone National Park)

Major Industries

Agriculture:

Sheep and cattle graze Montana's grasslands, where most crops are grown. Montana ranks especially high as a producer of wheat and barley.

Mining:

The state motto recalls Montana's fabulous mineral wealth, most of it in the mountainous west. The discovery of gold in 1852 sparked Montana's first great burst of growth, including such mining camps as Mannack (1862) and Virginia City (1864).

The "richest hill on earth," at present Butte, was the site of the discovery of silver in 1875 and copper sometime around 1880. Montana once supplied half the nation's copper, which played a major role in Montana history. Lead, zinc, and (in eastern Montana) coal and oil also contributed greatly to Montana's history and economy.

Tourism:

Montana's scenic beauty and vast empty spaces have made tourism its second largest industry.

History

Native Americans:

Sioux, Cheyenne, Blackfoot, Shoshone, Arapaho, Kootenai, and Flathead Indians inhabited Montana when Europeans first began to explore the territory. The Battle of Little Bighorn, probably the most famous of all "Indian battles," took place in 1876 in southeastern Montana. Sioux and Cheyenne warriors led by Crazy Horse and Sitting Bull massacred General George Custer and his entire command of more than two hundred men. The battle marked the end of the Plains Indian wars. In 1967 the Nez Percé, led by Chief Joseph, defeated the U.S. Army at Big Hole but were later captured by U.S. troops. Today, eleven tribes on seven reservations comprise roughly 7 percent of Montana's population.

Exploration and Settlement:

Louis-Joseph and François Verendrye first explored the area in the early 1740s. The Lewis and Clark expedition crossed Montana in 1805 on their historic trek to the Pacific Ocean. FranJois Antoine Laroque and his North West Company of Canada explored the Yellowstone River that same year. The first trading post in Montana was established at the mouth of the Bighorn River in 1807 by a trading expedition that Manuel Lisa led up the Missouri River from St. Louis.

Territory:

organized as Montana Territory on May 26, 1864
(previously part of the territories of Oregon, Washington, Nebraska, Dakota, and Idaho)

Statehood:

entered the union on November 8, 1889 (41st state)

Check It Out

For more information about the historical people and places in this book, check out the following books and web sites:

Montana

Web site: http://www.state.mt.us/

Crow Agency/Indian Reservations

Web site: http://tlc.wtp.net/crow.htm

Custer's Last Stand (Battle of the Little Bighorn)

Books: Stein, R. Conrad. *The Battle of the Little Bighorn.* Danbury, Conn.: Children's Press, 1997.

Herman, J. Viola, ed. *It Is a Good Day to Die.* Avenal, N.J.: Random House, 1998.

Web site:
http://www.mohicanpress.com/battles/ba04000.html

Glacier National Park

Web sites:
http://www.sd5.k12.mt.us/glaciereft/default.htm

http://www.nps.gov/glac/home.htm

Book: Patent, Dorothy Hinshaw. *Where the Bald Eagles Gather.* New York: Clarion Books, reprint 1990.

Grant-Kohrs National Historic Site

Web site: http://www.nps.gov/grko/

Lewis and Clark Expedition

Book: Bohner, Charles. *Bold Journey: West with Lewis and Clark.* New York: Houghton Mifflin Co., reprint 1990.

Web sites: http://www.amrivers.org/quizintro.html

http://www.lewisandclark.state.mt.us/

http://www.lewis-clark.org/

http://www.nationalgeographic.com/features/98/lewisclark/

http://www.pbs.org/lewisandclark/

Pompey's Pillar

Web site: http://www.mt.blm.gov/pompeys/index.html

Sacajawea

Books: Jassem, Kate. *Sacajawea Wilderness Guide.* Mahwah, N.J.: Troll Communications, 1997.

Rowland, Della. *The Story of Sacajawea: Guide to Lewis and Clark.* New York: Yearling Books, 1989.

Web sites: http://bi.uwyo.edu/news99/sacagawea.htm

http://www.pbs.org/weta/thewest/wpages/wpgs400/w4sacaga.htm

Join Ashley and Adam on their

South Dakota Treaty Search . . .

Ashley set the lamp on the picnic table and unfolded a comfortable lawn chair. She pulled mosquito netting down on the sides of the awning of the motor home. Sitting in the brisk air beneath the canopy of the dark South Dakota sky, a Native American quilt her mom had bought that day wrapped around her legs, Ashley opened her new book. The pages were yellow and stiff but in good condition. Ashley was tantalized immediately, reading about the very prairie on which she had walked that day. The book got right into the Indians' relationship with buffalo, and the family had seen lots of buffalo around Wind Cave.

Ashley read for quite a while, dozed, and read some more, closing in on page one hundred of the 340-page book. *Mom and Dad should be home soon,* she thought as she peeked inside the camper and saw Adam sleeping. The clock read 12:15 A.M., so she decided that she too should call it a night. The book wasn't going anywhere—Crazy Horse would be there in the morning, counting coup and giving ponies to those in his tribe who were needy or had none.

Flipping through the pages she'd read, Ashley felt the book's heft. She turned to the last page of the book to see how many pages were left to read. Noticing a break in the pages, Ashley gently held the book by its binding and slowly shook it back and forth. A piece of badly worn paper, not even four inches wide by five inches high, folded in half, fell out and drifted to the ground. It was much thicker than the pages of the book.

Ashley picked it up and held it closer to the light to get a better look. The lines were broken and no sentence was finished.

Quietly, she read each line: "On this 1st day of January, 1875 . . . America and all American Indians agree . . . which is binding here in this form, and will . . . days. This treaty finalizes all arrangements . . . and land rights to the Black Hills in the . . . until a time 10 years from now on the first . . . Nation is to assume full control of the Bla— . . . all land rights to the Black Hills. As of . . . allowed in the Black Hills. All rail lines . . . government, and all roads will be left to . . . see fit."

Unable to make sense of the fragmented writing, Ashley studied the first two hand-scrawled signatures below it. One was General C-something, but she couldn't make out the rest. The other signature was something *Gratton*. Below those were what looked like three signatures in a language that made no sense to Ashley. But what was this paper? Whose were the signatures? And where could the rest of the thing be? In the Black Hills somewhere? Maybe back home in Washington, D.C., with other U.S. government documents?

"Adam!" Ashley called, quickly hopping the stairs into the motor home.

Shaking off the deep sleep he had been enjoying only for an hour, Adam sat up and yawned. Ashley showed him the paper and breathlessly told him how it had fallen out of the book.

Adam yawned again.

"Quit yawning, this is exciting!" his sister shouted.

Just then, their parents pulled into the campground.

"Good! Maybe Mom and Dad will be awake enough to appreciate this!" Ashley said indignantly. Adam flopped back down on his bed.

Ashley showed the paper to her father and mother as soon as they came up the steps.

"What do you think it is?" Ashley asked.

"I don't know," her father answered. "Any thoughts, Anne?" Mr. Arlington gently placed the paper in the palm of his flat hand, sensing its brittleness.

"I don't know for sure," she said. She put on her glasses and guided her husband's hand under a light for a better look. "But if I had to guess, I'd say it looks like it might be part of a treaty."

A treaty! Ashley and Adam looked at each other in amazement. If it was signed according to the day in the lower left-hand corner, the document was 122 years old.

Ashley told the whole family what the clerk at the souvenir shop at Crazy Horse Monument had told her, about how a Sioux elder had bought the books from their original printing more than half a century ago.

"Were there other copies of the book at the shop?" Mrs. Arlington asked, her blond curls bobbing.

"Five in the store, plus this one," Ashley recalled, holding up her copy of the book.

Mr. Arlington smiled, a sparkle in his brown eyes. "As usual, our vacation is turning out to be very intriguing," he said. "Let's head back to the monument in the morning, first thing. We'll see if there are any more pieces to this puzzle."

What will the Arlingtons find when they return to the monument?

Watch for more books in the
X-Country Adventures series

Ashley and Adam Arlington have a knack for uncovering mysteries wherever they go—even while on vacation in the various states. Each book in this series presents a new puzzle for the Arlington siblings to solve.

0-8010-4453-7 $5.99

Crime in a
COLORADO Cave

✖ While visiting Cave of the Winds in Colorado, Ashley and Adam Arlington are caught up in the task of catching the thieves who steal a display of costly crystals from the cave's visitor center. The siblings use their observational skills and critical thinking to help the police officer on the case put the pieces together and recover the stolen crystals.

Adventure in WYOMING

0-8010-4452-9 $5.99

✖ When a family friend mysteriously disappears just hours after having served as their climbing guide, the Arlingtons set out to help in any way they can. Their sleuthing leads to more adventure than they bargained for, though, as they trek across the state on a clue-gathering mission that leads them to beautiful Yellowstone National Park.

Sports writer and newspaper editor **Bob Schaller** has won several awards for his journalistic excellence. Now a full-time writer, he is the author of The Olympic Dream and Spirit series, which covers athletes such as Mary Lou Retton, Dan O'Brien, Andre Agassi, and Dominique Moceanu. Schaller is also writing a biography of U.S. Olympic swimmer Amy Van Dyken. He lives in Colorado Springs, Colorado.